Jewel Thief

Flor Heis

Contents

Prologue

Elizabeth Murgatroyd sucked her thumb and squeezed her mother's hand tighter, gazing at her father who was wearing camouflage like the rest of them. The girl and her family were standing on a platform, and there was a huge crowd of men all in camouflage standing around, crying, and hugging their wives and children. "Why is Daddy leaving?" Madeleine Murgatroyd, Elizabeth's seven-year-old sister, had asked her mother, Isabel Murgatroyd. "Because the Germans are attacking and Daddy has to go help," she had said. "I'm sorry, sweetie. War is upon us."

Now Elizabeth stared at her father, her sister, her mother. She was three and didn't understand what was going on and what was going to happen. She continued to suck on her thumb, sucking until her mouth was red and hurt.

Suddenly, a train whizzed along the tracks and made Elizabeth's hair flap in the strong wind. She gasped in a toddler way and looked up at her mother. "Daddy has to leave now, Lizzy-B," her mother said slowly. "I'm sorry, darling."

As David Murgatroyd said his farewells to Madeleine (who was always called Maddie) and his wife, Elizabeth fiddled with her hair and thought about how she really fancied some chocolate. So Daddy was leaving for a bit. He would be back tomorrow, probably.

She understood suddenly that her daddy was leaving for a long time when he scooped her up into his arms and swung her about like he always did. But this time, he looked sad. Instead of putting her down, he held her in his arms and grinned, his eyes brimming with tears. "My girl, my little girl," he said. Elizabeth wrapped her arms around his head and put her head on him. When Elizabeth looked up, he looked into her eyes, smiled, and put her down. Then he knelt down and held her little hand.

"Don't you worry, Lizzy-B," he said, gently stroking her cheek with one finger as he spoke. "It's all going to be fine. I'm going to be back before you know it." He was really reassuring himself because Elizabeth didn't understand what was going on. "Everything is going to be okay."

He stared into the girl's eyes. "Promise me something, Elizabeth. Promise me that you will always stay strong and keep your chin up. Never give up hope on me. Do you promise?" His eyes twinkled, like they always did.

Elizabeth looked at her father, and after a while nodded slowly. She did understand what he was saying, and she would never forget what he said. Mr. Murgatroyd hugged Elizabeth one more time, whispering something into her ear.

"Wait for me, Lizzy-B. Wait for me."

And he turned towards the train and stepped up, glancing at Elizabeth with an expression unfamiliar to the little girl, which made her more con-fused than she already was. Then he got on, and the doors creaked closed behind him.

The train gradually got going, steam emitting from it. Mrs. Murgatroyd wiped her eyes and wept silently. Maddie crossed her arms and stared at her shoes, angry, confused and sad at the same time. She suddenly uncrossed her arms, lost in indecision, and began fiddling with the woven bracelet that her mother had just given her for her seventh birthday. But Elizabeth, little three-year-old Elizabeth toddled away from her family, across the platform, her hair once again flapping in the wind, towards the train that was speeding off into the distance. And then she stood there, watching, as the train slowly got further and further away, and she wondered if she would ever see her father again.

Leaving

NINE YEARS LATER

If you've ever been to one of the Earl's parties, you know a load of rubbish about us, the Murgatroyd sisters. The Earl always tells the same stories to all of his guests so that nobody knows the truth. To be honest, I can't really blame him because the truth is rather odd and sad, and also, I know that the Earl never wanted us to be his adopted children in the first place. So, if you have been to one of his parties (which I hate, because Maddie and I have to prepare for them all by ourselves, and he has them about once a month) I would prefer you knew our real story, not the big lie that we're his second cousins living in his house because our family is in prison. So listen to my story, and you shall find out.

Maddie and I are orphans. Yes, now you know that it's going to be sad. If you don't like sad things, then I advise you not to keep reading. Dad left to fight in 1943 when I was only three. We lived in London with Mum and Granny for a year, until one night in 1944 Mum had to go out to the hospital urgently to help some people who got injured, because she was a nurse. She didn't come back. Her body was never found, and nobody saw what happened to her but we still had a bit of a funeral for her around a fire, saying prayers. I was only four but I remember it very well. After that, we continued to live with Granny for a few months. During that time we got a telegram reporting Dad "missing in action', which means that they had no idea where he was and he was probably dead. I didn't think he was dead, though. Maddie says it was probably because I didn't really understand death, but I know that it was because Dad promised me he would come home. I believed that he was going to come home. But he didn't come home. And unfortunately, Granny died of a common sickness a few weeks later.

Maddie and I were taken to an orphanage, but one day Maddie and I snuck out to look at the war scene – my idea. I was five. It was rather idiotic, I have to admit – Maddie, who was nine at the time, tried to persuade me against it, in vain – but it turned out to be a life-saving idea. When we were just a little ways away, an air raid began. That meant the Germans were bombing again. Everyone started running down the stairs towards the bomb shelter. The manager of the orphanage screamed at us to get in the shelter with them. Maddie took my hand and ran back, pulling me along with her, but before the manager could even finish her sentence, a bomb hit the orphanage and everything was lost, including about fifty people and our records. They had been too late to get into the bomb shelter. At the time, I didn't know what records were, but Maddie explained to me that records were documents that had our backgrounds and information in writing, like who our parents were, if we were or were not fostered, things like that. Our birth certificates were in there as well, so there was no record of our names, or anything to do with our life. After the bomb hit, Maddie and I had nowhere to go. We lived on the streets for a few days, miserable and wondering what our lives were to become. We took refuge down in the tube stations with everyone during the air raids, sleeping on the cold, concrete floors, since we didn't have any blankets or bedding. Those nights were probably the worst of my life. When there were no air raids, we just sat on the streets, going numb from cold. This lasted maybe a month or two, since we completely lost track of time. Eventually, a nice lady who we later found out was named Charlotte Grayson spotted us.

She asked us what we were doing, which was looking for any food that was public domain – unlikely, nobody was about to feed a couple of random kids. Well, sometimes we looked so sad and forlorn that some people chucked coins at us, or threw us the rest of their rationed food (those were the happiest moments, and we tore at the food like wolves) I know you're not really supposed to talk to strangers, but we were really desperate and had no way of going to live with anyone else, so we had to trust her. We also told her our orphanage had been bombed, our Mum was dead, and Dad was M.I.A. Well, it was mostly Maddie who did the talking. I just sort of sat there and said a couple of silly things (I was five, it's no surprise). She seemed to be touched by the story that was so normal to us and kindly offered to let us stay with her (even though there was a war going on!) until we could find official guardians (mind you, we never did). So we went back to Kew Gardens with Charlotte, and Maddie and I were very glad we could live with this wonderful, kind woman. We thought things were going to be much better.

But Charlotte never mentioned that she was married to a man called Richard Grayson, although he goes by Earl Grayson (he isn't even a real earl, he just gave himself that title, to sound posh). He was upset with Charlotte for taking in "disgusting orphan street scum that would dirty his carpets", as he put it, without his approval. That was when I knew he wasn't going to be the best temporary father. Even now he only calls me "girl" (that's when he's not cross, it can easily be "idiot" or "orphan girl" [that really puts me off] when he's angry or even just in a slightly bad mood) instead of my name, Elizabeth. At least Charlotte was kind to Maddie and me, and in her presence, the Earl tried to be okay as well. Unfortunately, she died an untimely death in 1949 (the Earl said she had had a heart attack and left it at that) and left us alone with the horrible man. Maddie and I basically became unpaid, unofficial servants. When we address him we have to call him "sir." Not "Mr. Grayson." Not "Earl Grayson." And, of course, not Richard. He said it would be an insult to him if we, the ridiculous homeless orphan gits that his wife had scooped up off the street, called him by his first name. Every time he brings this up, which is a lot because sometimes we say it just to annoy him when he's already too cross to become any crosser, I can't help but roll my eyes.

Now it's 1952 and we're still here, in Kew Gardens. Dad still hasn't come home. I bring the Earl meals, sweep the floors, do cleaning in general, and be formal at all times (not that I would want to be anything else except harsh). Is he stuck in the Edwardian times or something? I feel like Cinderella sometimes. And we don't go to school. The Earl says it costs too much but I think he really just wants us around to do chores and wait on him. And, of course, he doesn't pay us because whenever we (courageously) bring up possible payment/allowance, he gets cross and says that he didn't employ me, he was my guardian, and children typically "help around the house". Maddie and I do more than help.

During the week, he does work, but he's never bothered to tell me what his job is. He only works four hours a day, and when he comes back, he expects the house to be absolutely immaculate. He is very strict about cleanliness, and he gets cross at as when there is a single speck of dirt. That's too much for girls our age, if you ask me. He punishes me awfully when he finds that it's too dirty. It's terrible. Once he locked me up in my room for three days, without food (he would slip small glasses of water under my door), because I had missed the spare room when I cleaned. I hadn't slept well the night before! It's not that much of a problem! Maddie had had to stay in the spare room that I had missed during that time, and the Earl threw a load of rubbish on the floor of the room to make it extra squalid for her, and also so that next time I cleaned, I would have an extra job. Plus I didn't have her company that night, so I felt incredibly lonely. At least I got out of cleaning for three days, but I felt really guilty that Maddie had to work extra hard those three days because I wasn't helping. Another time, I had made an effort to thoroughly clean, after the dreadful spare room experience, but he made an awful comment after he had investigated the house. I remember him coming down the stairs to where I was waiting for him. He looked to both sides and then at me. Then he said "Well, no, it's not clean. Because there's still this filth holding a broom, standing right in front of me!" – gesturing towards me. I didn't come out of my bedroom the whole rest of that evening. I had worked so hard, and, in return, he calls me filthy!

Maddie has different jobs, but we're barely allowed to see each other during the day so I don't know what they are. We whisper constantly of the day's hardships at night, but it would be ridiculous to talk about our jobs, we have more important things to discuss. But we get caught chatting late into the night sometimes, and if we do, the Earl duct tapes our mouths (it's a new kind of tape, the Earl has some) and locks the door until morning. Sometimes we think of Dad, and if he will ever come back. I still secretly believe that he will, but I don't tell Maddie. She would think it "highly implausible", and then give me a whole load of reasons why, like she does all the time. I feel stupid to feel like this is a "hardship". I'm sure that if Dad came back and told us about the war, he would have far, far worse stories. But I still think our story is quite interesting – if you're not me or Maddie. For us, it's just one terrible thing after another, beginnings that end too quickly.

The only things to comfort me while we live here with the Earl, besides Maddie of course, are my books. Mystery books, to be exact. You might think that they must have been destroyed by the orphanage bomb, but we always carried the money that Granny gave us in her will. So we had enough money to buy more, and Charlotte let us have others later on, although mine were directed towards nine-year-olds, so now I read ones meant for Maddie previously – she was thirteen when Charlotte bought books for her. She and I both have loads of different kinds of mysteries now, from simple robberies to murders. My favorite author is Enid Blyton. She wrote loads of different series, and she didn't just write mysteries, but my favorite of hers is the Famous Five. It's about a group of four children and a dog named Timothy who run about solving mysteries and then get really famous for having solved them. The best character is George, a plucky, tomboyish girl whose real name is Georgina but she hates it – too girly, and I think so too – so everybody has to call her George. Maddie and I both really love reading.

There we go, that's my life in a nutshell.

Apart from the books, life is horrid here, and Maddie and I both know it. We always talk of perhaps running away, but we have nowhere to go to. We can't exactly walk up to an orphanage and demand they take us in, either. We have no relatives that we know of. And we don't have any money to pay for ships or anything. We're pretty much stuck here. I don't know what we're going to do next. But I'm twelve now, twelve two months ago, and I need a change.

I think about this as I clean – well, attempt to clean – Earl Grayson's desk. It's a complete and utter mess. There are pens scattered everywhere, a week-old coffee mug (I know because I remember bringing it to him) is tipped over and there's a dried-up brown stain left from it that he wants me to tidy up, there are some papers lying around all higgledy-piggledy, and to top it all off, he spilled blue ink all over many papers and important-looking things. I sigh, shuffling a stack of undamaged papers together and stowing them away at the back of the desk.

Suddenly, I spot something under the pile of papers that I just moved. It was a little yellow piece of paper, quite worn and crumpled, as if it had been there a long time. And on it, in familiar script, was something that wanted to make me cry out, I was so ecstatic:

'9/12/1949

Maddie and Elizabeth's Uncle's (Henry Murgatroyd) address:

2578 Eleanor Lane NE

Middle-Rose Square

Long Island, NY 45934

USA

~ C.G.'

C.G. stood for Charlotte Grayson. She always signed documents like that. And, from the date on the paper, she had written on it very, very shortly before she died.

We had an Uncle. Our parents' will said to leave us with any relative possible. And here was his address.

We were going to go to the United States of America.

I completely abandon the disastrous desk and rush to find Maddie. After running through the hall and the kitchen (I went around the living room, for that was where the Earl was sure to be), I eventually locate her on the patio, sweeping up the gathered dust there, her cheeks flushed from all the hard work set upon us.

"Maddie!" I cry, waving the little slip of paper in her face. "You'll never believe what I found."

She looks up from her sweeping, visibly surprised that I had so abruptly left my work to come tell her something.

"What is it?" she asked in a low, tired voice. Then she yawns. "Aren't you supposed to be cleaning something somewhere?"

I look at her, my face suddenly anxious.

"Maddie, are you all right? You really don't look good."

She slumps down on the patio chair. "Yes, I'm fine. Just overworked, I suppose."

I frown, unsure that this was all. "Did you get enough sleep?"

"Yes, Elizabeth. Really, I'm okay. Now hurry up and tell me what you have to say – the Earl's going to come and find us and get really cross."

I sigh, nodding. There's no need for her to remind me of the precautions I must take. But my elated mood returns almost instantly.

"Well, anyways, I have fabulous news! Look at this piece of paper!" I exclaim, thrusting the paper at her. She tucks her hair behind the rim of her glasses like she always does when she's about to read something. I watch as her expression suddenly goes from tired to surprised to euphoric.

"WHAT? He's alive? I remember, Dad used to talk about him! We went to visit him once, in 1939, before you were born! Dad seemed really cross at him before he left for war. I think they had an argument. I thought he was dead. But he's alive? I can't believe it!"

I didn't know that Maddie had already met him, but I didn't really care. I was overjoyed, and all other thoughts were blocked out. "Yes! Now we have to live with him, because of the law! Because of Mum and Dad's will!"

"We lawfully have to live with him?"

"Yes! Remember the will?" I know that part off by heart. "Ahem – we also desire that our – er... what is it again? Oh yeah – our daughters go to a relative who is able to take them in most convieniently."

"That's fabulous!" she cries, her eyes no longer droopy, but shining in delight. "We should go tell the Earl about it right now."

"Right now? But won't he punish us?"

"He's not technically our guardian anymore! We don't have to listen to him!"

"That's a good point," I say, a grin spreading onto my face.

But what if he doesn't listen to us? nags a little voice in the back of my head. I ignore it, too overjoyed to listen to my better conscience.

Maddie and I run off the patio, through the hall, and into the sitting room, where the Earl was sitting comfortably on his favorite armchair. It was pristine and polished. The whole room was pristine and polished. In fact, you could say that the Earl resembled his house a lot. There were stiff wooden chairs circling the fireplace that was never lit. There was a table in the corner also made of wood, very clean and shiny and more polished as usual, for I had just cleaned it that morning for the umpteenth time. There was a wooden grandfather clock propped up against the wall, ticking noisily and sharply. Everything looked stiff and sharp and strict. The walls were a grotesque yellow color, and the paint was peeling tremendously. There were pictures on the wall – all in dull wooden frames – and they were all of the Earl. There used to be some of him and Charlotte, but when she died he took them down and hid them in the basement.

The Earl looks up from the newspaper he was scrutinizing when he heard us and immediately frowns. The corner of his black moustache twitches. He draws the pipe out of his mouth, scowling.

"What are you orphan girls doing here? You're supposed to be cleaning! Get out!"

I was very accustomed to the rude behavior of the Earl, so I was not taken aback at all. But I was insulted by him calling me an orphan, that's always the worst insult you can give me. Go ahead, call me an idiot, call me useless, call me a disgusting filthy wretch (all of which have been used by the Earl), but call me an orphan and I will not be happy.

"Actually, sir, I found something whilst cleaning your horridly untidy desk. Look!"

I hold out the piece of paper to him and he snatches it out of my hand, scowling.

"What is this rubbish?"

I was surprised that he was not cross about the comment I slipped in about his desk, but I didn't let it bother me. In fact, it was good.

"Just look!" I say again. "Charlotte found our Uncle's address! He's our legal guardian! In our parents' will, they said that we had to go to the nearest relative. We have to go there according to the law."

The Earl observes the piece of paper, the lines in his face creased. I could tell he was highly irritated by this development. Then he crumples it up and throws it on the floor. I gasp and quickly picked it up, smoothing it out. We couldn't lose it, or else we wouldn't have the address anymore.

"I don't care about your stupid will. You don't actually have it, do you?"

Maddie and I exchange a look. Neither of us had remembered that we had no proof that this was in the will. We needed to present the actual will to him. Then, and only then, would it be lawful.

Luckily for me, Maddie speaks up. It surprises me, since I know she was secretly very frightened of him as well.

"Well, er... yes, it was destroyed when the orphanage was bombed. But we remember what it said! And besides, it's not like you ever wanted us around. You don't love us. And we want to leave. Once in your life, Richard, do something kind for us. It's not like we wanted to end up here! To be honest with you, and I think Elizabeth quite agrees, I would probably rather live on the street than with you, now that the war's long since finished. So let us leave. It's not expensive to get a ship to America. And he lives in New York – from what I remember, that's on the coast. If you hate us so much, why didn't you get rid of us earlier?"

I stare at Maddie. She had a lot of courage to stand up to the Earl like that. And she called him Richard. The Earl was going to be really cross.

Sure enough, the Earl's face goes very red. He gives her the Death Glare (that's what Maddie and I call the face he makes when we're about to be in very, very, very deep trouble), so I know things are not good. He sets down his newspaper as hard as he could – which wasn't very hard, giving it was a newspaper – and rose to his feet, still giving Maddie the Death Glare. Then he said, in a low, furious tone:

"How dare you. How dare you speak to me like that. Is it impossible to get any respect around here? Authorizing yourselves to use my first name! You are unbelievable. Get back to work at once."

I tug on Maddie's arm. "Maddie, stop," I whisper. "I can take it from here. You shouldn't get into any more trouble!"

"Oh, I dare," Maddie says proudly in response to Uncle, completely ignoring me. "Because in a few days, we're not going to live with you anymore."

"Madeleine Emily Murgatroyd! Go back to your work immediately! Get out of my sight! That goes for you too!" He points at me.

Uh-oh. He's passed to Stage 2, which is when he calls us by our full names – and by full, I mean full, middle name and all. And he pretty much never calls us by our names. We told him our full names when we first met, and he clearly remembers, although he never uses them apart from Stage 2 of his anger.

"Maddie, stop talking! He's only going to get crosser," I warn, hushing my voice.

She ignores me again, giving Uncle a cold stare. "Give us one reason why you want us around. And it has to be a good reason. All right?"

"You do not have the authority to order me around like this!" he shouted. "Did you hear me? Get out and go back to work."

"I'm sort of an adult now," she reminds him. "Remember? I was sixteen last month."

He scowls. "You may be almost an adult," he said, "but I'm still in charge around here!"

"Give us a reason," Maddie repeated.

"All right, here's your reason – you are helpful and I can't do all the work around here alone. There. Now get out. This is the last time I shall tell you!"

"That's a ridiculous reason!" I exclaim, joining the argument as I realize that now that the Earl was cross, you could fight back as much as you wanted. One of my mottos is to choose what you fight for, and this is something I want to fight for. "You just want us as servants to His Royal Highness, is that correct? And I think it's more won't than can't. It's not that hard to hire a maid! Or, you could actually do the work by yourself. Does that sound so diffi-"

"Elizabeth Annabella Murgatroyd!"

"Children aren't supposed to be cooped up in a house doing all the chores! We're supposed to be going to school! School! Elizabeth was only nine when she stopped schooling!" Maddie cries.

The Earl resumes the Death Stare and starts tapping his foot. Oh no. Stage 3. Shouting time was coming up.

"ALL RIGHT!" he roars. "YOU CAN GO TO AMERICA! JUST DON'T EXPECT ME TO GO WITH YOU!"

I stare at the Earl, wondering if this was a dream or if I was mishearing him. Maddie stares with me, and then we exchange a glance. We're both lost for words – this was the first time either of us could remember him ever agreeing to do something for us. Yes, okay, he had gone through all stages of anger and shouted at us, but nevertheless... we were leaving the Earl, forever.

The Earl's face was still blotchy red. He coldly stared at us for what seemed like an eternity, before speaking very quietly.

"Elizabeth, go finish tidying my desk. Madeleine, sweep the patio. I do not want to hear a word from you little wretches the rest of the day. I shall arrange you for a boat trip to New York City in two days time. And Elizabeth, no supper for you either. You are to do as you are told the whole remainder of the time you are here, or you shall not leave. Understood?"

"Yes, sir," Maddie says, breathless. We scurry off to our tasks, grinning. I barely register that he actually used our names.

We exchange a glance.

A new life was beginning.

A Boat and Molly

- -

In two days it is time to board the boat that shall take us to America. It is called the Queen Mary, apparently. We get a train to Southampton with the Earl, which was very interesting. We go right out of London, and rode all the way through the suburbs. Then there was countryside and plains. The Earl sits there giving us dirty looks whenever we made eye-contact, which Maddie and I don't mind in the least, because we read books the whole way. The fare was two pounds per person, and the Earl had to provide this money, which I know he was not happy about.

When the train arrives in Southampton, we see the boat. It is absolutely enormous. I can't see how so many people would want to travel to New York in one week. There are so many windows, and smoke billows out of the top. There is a deck, where early boarders are mingling, waving to the people on the dock. A big United States flag flutters in the wind. Maddie and I exchange a glance. Apart from the big buildings in central London, I don't think either of us had ever seen something so big. I can see the captain's cabin up top, and below deck were clearly the cabins we were to be living in. People's heads stuck out of the little windows. There are two masts at the front and back, but they looked pathetic compared to the size of the boat. It honked and emitted smoke and steam, and I cough. It looked a bit like an enormous washbasin. Emblazoned on the side was QUEEN MARY. The Earl had tried to frighten us beforehand by warning us that it had history of being haunted, but he didn't even know the tales, so it didn't scare me. It was a bit ominous, and it cast a huge shadow over the dock. It smelled like rancid fish, which was not a pleasant smell.

The Earl leaves without even a goodbye, although I don't know why I was expecting it. I bet he's really upset that he has nobody to wait on him anymore. I hastily try to muffle my laugh at the thought of this, coming out with a strange snort that gets a raised eyebrow from Maddie.

At the dock our names get called:

"Murgatroyd, Elizabeth," calls the captain. "Present," I answer. "Murgatroyd, Madeleine," he calls again. "Present," replies Maddie. And the list goes on.We get on the great rocking ship and I prepare to never see England again. I am happy to leave the smoggy Thames and dirty streets but I have lived here my whole life. It is terribly sad.

Maddie says we shall return to England, but I am not so sure. Not if there are any more World Wars. Sometimes I think about the whole prospect of World War III. It scares me, but I don't think about it long.

It takes about an hour for everyone to board. We have loaded all our things, and settled into our miniature cabin, with a marvelous bunk bed in the corner. I have the top bunk! It is quite a squeeze and the toilets are on deck, very far away, but I am sure I will enjoy myself. At least, I think. When Dad left for the war, I remember him making me promise to keep my chin up and look on the bright side, but I have never been on a ship before. And it really does smell like fish gone off. The floorboards creak underneath my feet, and I wonder how I'm possibly going to sleep on this thing with the constant tossing of the waves. No matter how big the boat, you're always tossed about by the ever-powerful monster of the ocean.

Everyone shares a room with one other person, and if you were in a group of three or more, you got separated. Normally adults were with adults, and children were with children. There are mostly children on this ship. I know this because when the captain was reading the rooming statistics on the dock I was bored so I listened to everything he was saying.

The ship is setting sail! We steal a chance to go on deck and see our last glimpse of England. I blink back tears, hugging my sister. The dock is full of parents and relatives waving goodbye. Of course, none of them are ours.

"We will be back – I'm sure of it." Maddie comforts me again, but I can hear her voice breaking – she's near tears. The Southampton dock is becoming a small blob. The parents are getting smaller and smaller... gone.We head back downstairs. I sit down on my bed hugging my knees together, and Mr. Bearface, my old teddy, at the same time. I know it's a bit of a ridiculous name for a teddy, and I'm really a bit old for teddies, but I was three when I named him, and besides, he's the only memory I have of Mum. He is dark brown, and he is wearing a faded dark green-and-red colored jumper with a bonnet to match. I smile at his fuzzy face. I have had him since I can remember because apparently he was given to Mum before I was born. Maddie says I am too old for teddies but that is only because she is jealous since she does not have one herself. At least, that's what Mum told me when I came to her crying eight years ago that Maddie was teasing me about him. I sigh. I miss Mum so much.

I lie on my bed with Mr. Bearface for the next half-hour, trying to remember everything I can about London. I end up remembering how sad I felt when I learned that Mum had died and later that Dad was gone. I sigh. The memories that I had thought of definitely failed to make me feel better about leaving here.

My mind returns to the present day, in our little cabin, where Maddie is tidying her clothes neater than necessary in the tiny cabinet. I grin. She is such a perfectionist. I fidget awhile and then decide to go explore. I tell Maddie where I am going and climb down off the bed. I walk around a bit but then I hear weeping. I see a little girl no more than nine crying on her bed. I walk up to her.

'What's wrong?" I ask.

"I-I miss my Daddy. H-He died in the L-Lynmouth Flood. V-Very recently. My M-Mummy got hit by a b-bomb during t-the w-war when I was just a-a little baby. Now I have to go live with my gr-granddad in A-America." She sniffs. "My – my name is Molly Ashburne," she tells me, gaining confidence. "I'm nine and a half. What's your name?"

"Elizabeth. Elizabeth Annabella Murgatroyd. I'm twelve and two months, thirteen in June next year. And I'm really sorry about your parents. Mine are dead too, you're not alone." I smile at her. It used to be difficult to think of Mum and Dad. But now I'm so used to being an orphan that I don't really mind bluntly bringing it up.

Molly Ashburne wipes away her tears, beaming at me. "I'm sorry too. Oh, and this is William, my roommate. His parents died in a car accident recently." Molly said casually as if William had been none other than a schoolmate.

I go up to a boy around seven, also crying and much harder, and put my hand on his back. "Are you all right?" But he doesn't reply. Maybe he prefers talking to a nine-year-old girl than a twelve year old one, as he appears to have told Molly about his backstory. I offer to take him and Molly along on my explorations of the boat. Molly says yes but William declines.

We decide to explore the deck and the ship's front. We wander around up top, sighting the toilets and securing its location in our brain. We are to live here for a week, at the least. We find ourselves up front and look at the view. We are sailing around the bottom of England, so we can reach the wide Atlantic to get to America.

I stand next to her, looking out at the distant blob of land that the captain says is France. I want to go to France, but I don't know any French. Languages interest me, though. I was about to take up Spanish with Charlotte right before she died, but there was no time.

"Annabella's a pretty middle name," Molly suddenly comments. "My middle name is Ariana. After my great-grandmother."

"Molly Ariana Ashburne is a nice name. And Ashburne's a nice last name. I don't really like Murgatroyd. People spell it wrong a lot. My sister, Maddie, is Madeleine Emily Murgatroyd, which I find to be much nicer."

"You have a pretty name," she says again. We look back out at the sea. France is fading into the distance. I sigh.

I leave Molly back in her room, and I head back to my room to talk to Maddie.I go down to sit next to her on her bed and we have a long conversation about London and our memories. This was not a very uplifting conversation, since all of the happy things in my life ended abruptly at some point and when I thought about them, it made me sad to think that that life was gone. I do not mention the memory of Mum going out and never returning, or any other bad memories of the war. Neither does Maddie.

After this, it is time for supper. They have us all sit at this incredibly long table. There are the tiniest portions of canned beans and bread with margarine. It might sound rather awful to you, but believe it or not, this is better than what we normally got at the Earl's. We finish this off and then the captain gives us a speech about our trip. He talks about how excited he is to have us on this journey and he hopes we enjoy it also. He's a bit too cheery for my liking. We walk back to our bedrooms around nine-thirty, yawning.

I take a trip to the bathroom to brush my teeth but there is a long line so I don't bother. Maddie doesn't either. I pull on my thin nightgown and clamber into my high bed. "Goodnight," whispers Maddie from below. "Sleep well, Elizabeth."

"Goodnight," I lean down and whisper back, switching off my lamp. But sleep doesn't come fast. The power of the ocean keeps me awake for at least an hour, tossing me about and tangling me up in the paper-thin sheets.

It was going to be a tough journey to America.

The Lady and the Attic

After a few days of living on this thing I am already sick of it. We barely get anything to eat and there is nothing to do. The nice captain tries to stay optimistic about it but already he seems a bit weary. I spend most of the time lounging on deck. We are in the Atlantic Ocean, but I like to call it the Sea of Certain Doom. Why? Because it is frightening to see that there is no land visible as far as the eye can see. In all directions. It is just us, the ship, and the water. No land. I wonder if we will ever see it again.

Tomorrow we leave this place! Land has finally appeared very far off in the distance, and the captain says we will land in about eight hours. I am going to miss dear Molly lots, because she is my only friend besides Maddie. She has given me her address so I will write to her lots. I am becoming not so sure I want to live with my Uncle Henry, but now I have no choice. I pack up my satchel and make sure that Mr. Bearface is comfortable. I introduced him to Molly last night and she loved him. She showed me her stuffed rabbit, and he is very cute. Maddie is again unnecessarily re-folding her clothes ever so neatly. Maybe she is just anxious about Uncle. We are here! Before we dock we see an amazing statue. It is very big and is a lady holding up a torch in the air. It is very tall and is on a little island in the sea. We sail past it and finally land. Wow, America is fantastic. And busy.

A lot like London, but tidier. MUCH tidier. And there are huge, very tall buildings. It is very different. Everyone speaks in a funny accent. It sounds a bit Western, almost Australian. It is funny to think England used to rule this place.I give Molly an extremely large squeeze. She has more tears trickling down her cheeks. I know she is sad to leave us, so I say we will definitely visit. She rushes up to her very kind-looking granddad and tells him about me and gives him my address. He also gives me their address. I introduce myself, and he smiles. I give Molly one last hug and then rush to join Maddie. Pointing at a strange man, she leans down and whispers something into my ear: 'That's Uncle. We met him with Mum and Dad. You won't remember, you weren't even born. I barely remember it myself. He is very strict and doesn't like children very much, I don't think. Oh, and he used to have a wife, but she died a few years ago.' I groan. He doesn't like children? Is this going to be a repeat of the dreadful Earl?

Looking where she is pointing, I see my first glimpse of Uncle Henry. He is a tall, wiry-looking man wearing a classy white shirt and fancy black trousers. He has very hollow cheeks. He is scowling. I gulp. I do not want to live with this man! We slowly walk towards him and tell him who we are. He grunts 'hello' and takes us by the hands, pulling us away from the dock. I glance one last time at Molly, still chattering to her granddad. She sees me and waves. I smile. Uncle pulls us to a large, white car in excellent shape. I gasp. I have never ridden in one before, let alone use one regularly as we shall now do. He ushers us in and shuts the door.

The experience of riding in a car is entirely new to me. I had been on a train, but this is different. The world rushed by me, turning the trees and houses into blurry swirls of color. Then when Uncle slowed down, it was as if I was at walking speed. And sometimes the car was cruising slowly, so it was like I was running.

It feels odd, and my tummy ached. I ask Uncle if it would always be like this when we drove. 'No,' he says, 'you're just not used to it.' And that was that. I establish that Uncle was not a man of many words, but I could just be jumping to conclusions.

I start to feel slightly giddy, and my tummy ache goes away. This is so exciting! I hope we get to ride in the car a lot! I grin like a twit at Maddie. She grins back. I think we're both feeling the same. Of course, Uncle is unmoved. I bet he's enormously used to having a car. I narrow my eyes at him. I don't know why, but I've come to hate Uncle. Already.

It takes us a while to drive us across the island and over a large bridge to another island, but eventually, Uncle drives up to a beautiful, pale yellow house.

I gaze at it in wonder. The house is gorgeous, with a well-trimmed lawn in front and a little pathway leading to the front door. There is a window above the door, supposedly leading to the living room, with white walls. There seem to be two armchairs, one dark brown and tall, the other a similar color to the house itself, and stout. I assume the brown one is his and that the yellow one belonged to his wife. I do feel sorry for him about that.

In the window, there is also a large sofa, a cabinet – 'That cabinet rings a bell,' Maddie says – and something box-shaped, covered in a black tarp. I wonder what is under it.

Another window, next to the first, leads to a pale blue room, with two twin beds side by side. The beds look rather new, with clean white sheets neatly tucked in. I think I see a cupboard on the wall as well, but I am not sure, seeing as I am looking through the window from the car.

The only problem with the house is that it doesn't feel very homely. It seems as if it's looming over our car. I actually miss the Earl's house, as I have gotten used to it over the past seven years.

Uncle opens the car door and steps out. I almost expect him to open the door for us, but he walks right by and goes to walk up the path. I don't want to look like an idiot, so I open the door. Maddie is already walking towards the house. 'Hurry up, Elizabeth!' she says just as I am opening the door. I roll my eyes and run to join them.

Uncle pulls out a little key and lifts it up to the door, but he stops right as he's about to put it in the hole. He draws it away from the door, straightens his back and clears his throat. A speech was approaching, I could tell. I braced myself for him to drone on about house rules and whatnot.

"So, erm... welcome to my house, where you shall be living. I wish for you to keep to yourselves during the day, and for you to follow any rules I set, or there shall be consequences. I am your legal guardian, so you must respect me in the same way you would if I was your father." Yeah right, I think to myself. He goes on. "Your room is the blue bedroom upstairs that you might have noticed from outside." He points to the room with the blue walls that I saw through the window. "Oh, and the attic is off-limits. There could be broken glass on the floor, and I do not want to have to take you to hospital." He pauses to think. "That is all. You may go up to your room when we go in. And come down for supper at half past seven."

I shiver. He says it all in a calm, almost unctuous tone that I do not enjoy. I hope he does not speak like that all the time.

He finally unlocks the door and I slowly go in, gazing up at the beautiful house around me. There are pictures on the wall, of Uncle, of a lady, supposedly of his old wife, and I notice a boy in the background of one that I don't recognize. I also spot some less recent pictures of two boys – Uncle and... Dad. They were brothers. It was a wonder, considering, from what Maddie tells me, they were absolutely nothing alike.

Maddie walks next to me, with Uncle behind us. We pad over to the staircase and step up onto the first stair, still looking around at all of the pictures. There are loads, including one of Uncle getting married. He actually looks happy. It's strange to look at a picture of him smiling, for he hadn't smiled once since we had met.

When we get to the top, I look around at the doors, trying them to see which one is ours. I open the door to the bathroom, the study... and finally, I open a door that leads to the blue bedroom that I had seen from the car. The clock on the wall says 7:00. We have a half-hour to get settled. I take the bed closet to the door and that leaves Maddie with the one next to the window. I sit down on my new bed and face Maddie.

"I will find it difficult to get used to this place," I whisper, "it is rather fancy for me."

"I'm always here for you, Elizabeth. I feel awfully sorry for that girl Molly - at least her granddad seemed nice."

"Yes, he did seem kind."

We sit in silence for a moment. Then I get an idea.

"I am going to write to her – I miss her already."

I take out my favorite purple sparkly notebook that I was given by Charlotte years ago and tear out a page. Quickly, I scrawl out a letter to M olly.'Dear Molly, I am missing you lots! Uncle is strict but his house is magnificent. It is rather frightening though and does not feel homely. That's all for the moment. Write soon! Love, Elizabeth.'I fold the note in half, slip it in an envelope and scribble her address. I still know it off by heart, because she told me what it was about half an hour ago. Then I read a book for a while. After thirty minutes, Uncle calls for us. We go downstairs. He leads us into the dining room in silence and seats us in small chairs in front of a medium serving of mini breakfast sausages and - mashed potatoes? I've never had them before. They're supposed to be rather nice.

I slowly scoop up a small spoonful of them and put them in my mouth. They are probably the best things I have ever eaten. I shovel down mouthful after mouthful, barely stopping to chew, until I finish them. I have some sausages and then excuse myself from the table. Maddie calls my name but I head upstairs towards our room.

I am at the top of the stairs when I hear someone knock on the door. Who would possibly come calling at this time of night? I turn around to see Uncle walk out of the dining room and over to the door.

I take the stairs back down two at a time. He turns the door handle. I notice he looks as puzzled as I am. I walk over next to him as the door opens to reveal a young woman, about twenty-two. She looks a bit like a doll, with her bright blonde hair falling loosely over her shoulders. She is wearing a red dress with a huge, bouncy skirt at the bottom. A leopard-skin shawl is draped over her shoulders. She has red high-heels to match her red nails and bright-red lips. And her rather round, large eyes are covered in blue eyeshadow to make them look even bigger than they already are. In all, it is a very red outfit, except for the leopard-skin and blue eyeshadow. But apart from the obvious fashion obsession, she appears to be quite a nice lady.

"Hello! I recently moved into the neighborhood and I've been going around meeting my neighbors! I'm sorry for bursting in on you."

Uncle shakes his head. "Oh, not at all! Do come in."

"Thank you. I shall only be a minute." The lady smiles. It is an odd smile, and I can't help noticing something funny about it – something to do with her eyes. She glances over at me and for a brief moment, her smile falters. But then she looks back at Uncle, smile as big as ever.

"Not a problem!" Uncle told her.

The woman follows Uncle into the room, and he gestures to a comfortable armchair.

"I'm Marissa, by the way."

"Very nice to meet you, Marissa."

They sit down and start talking about whatever you talk about when a complete stranger comes to your door and introduces herself. At that moment, Maddie came in from the kitchen. She's a slow eater.

"What's all the commotion about?" She asks.

"Oh, a woman named Melissa – no, Marissa – just came to say that she recently moved here, and then Uncle invited her in, so..." I don't have to say any more. Maddie looks over towards Uncle and the lady and nods. I sigh.

"I think they're going to be there for a bit, unfortunately. Let's go get our books, and then sit on the sofa so we can eavesdrop." I add this last bit in a whisper and then grin.

Maddie giggles. "Okay. We don't have anything else to do, really."

We race each other upstairs. Marissa's arrival seems to have eased the tension, because staying in a house solely with Uncle is a bit intimidating. Snatching up an old, tattered book that I have read through many a time, I creep back downstairs and sit on a chair behind Uncle and the lady so that I can listen to what they're saying. I open my book and pretend to be reading, but really, I'm listening to what they're saying. Maddie joins me seconds later and proceeds to do exactly what I'm doing.

The conversation going on between Uncle and Marissa really is quite dull. By the time they have moved on to American politics, Maddie and I are actually reading our books, even though we'd read them a thousand times and had almost memorized them word-for-word – there was a period when we only had one book each at our disposal.

For some reason, I tune in when Marissa says, "Would you mind showing me to the restroom?"

Uncle responds "It's right upstairs, on the right."

She nods. "I'll only be a minute," she says, and starts on up the stairs.

While she is gone, Uncle sits silently on the armchair and awaits her return. I roll my eyes. Does he really have nothing else to do?

Maddie and I sit on the armchairs, conversing, but still paying attention to Uncle and the guest. Marissa is taking a long time on the toilet. Uncle seems to think so too, so he calls up "Are you all right, Marissa? You seem to be taking quite a long time."

There is a strange noise, and then a muffled voice comes from upstairs. "My apologies, Henry, I'll be right down." A few moments pass, and then I hear her high heels on the stairs. She reaches the landing and smiles at Uncle again. "It's about time I left, Mr. Murgatroyd. It's been a pleasure to meet you."

Uncle smiles again. "Of course, Marissa. It was so nice to have you in our home." I roll my eyes.

He shows Marissa to the door. She is about to leave, but then Uncle stops her on the threshold. "Would you like my telephone number, Marissa? So we can get in touch sometime soon?"

Marissa looks slightly bemused for a moment, but then she nods.

"Of course. I would love to." It seems to me that she sounds ever so slightly sarcastic.

Uncle takes out a notepad, scrawls something on it, tears it out of the book, and hands it to Marissa. "My number. Call me something soon, and we can figure something out, all right? I'm sure the girls would love to meet you properly."

Marissa's smile doesn't seemt so genuine anymore. She thanks Uncle for the number and leaves brusquely, shutting the door behind her.

Uncle's smile persists as he turns back to us. "Sorry for that minor disturbance, girls. But Marissa seems like a very nice lady, and I would love to get in touch with her again." He looks at his watch. "It's half past eight. I would like for you to be in bed by nine fifteen – both of you," he adds when Maddie begins to protest that she's sixteen and should go to bed at ten o'clock. "Oh, and Maddie, I would like you to help me with the dishes. Elizabeth, it shall be your turn tomorrow night, and we shall alternate every night."

Maddie turns to follow Uncle back into the kitchen. She waves at me, and I dash back up the stairs to my new room, so I could unpack and read some more books.

I stop near the bedroom. Above my head is a trapdoor that must lead to the attic. I don't care what Uncle says about broken glass. There must be something up there that's interesting. I see a ladder tucked carefully behind a cupboard, heave it over and lean it up against the flap. Nobody will hear me, kitchen is far away on the first floor. I slowly begin to climb it. It wobbles. I stop, my heart thumping in my chest. Ladders have always been a bit of an issue for me. The ladder is sturdy again so I take a deep breath and keep climbing.

I reach the trapdoor and slowly lift it. It reveals a dark, musky place, the air smelling of paint, with eerie-looking boxes, chests, abandoned furniture, and a dusty window in one corner. I close it and I am about to descend the ladder, since the attic is so boring, but then something catches my eye. The light from a window catches a small chest tucked deep in one corner of the attic, covered in cobwebs, with a keyhole. Is that what he's hiding?

I am about to climb up into the attic to see but I hear footsteps. Uncle is coming upstairs. Oh no.

I panic and the ladder wobbles again. I have some time, as the staircase is at the far end of the corridor that winds around to reveal the trapdoor. I race back up the ladder, lift the flap, climb back in the attic and slam the door. Looking through a small hole in the floor, I can see everything that is going on under me. Uncle stops at the ladder, mutters something under his breath, and moves on.

I exhale, not realizing that I had been holding my breath. My gaze turns back to the old, red chest hiding in the corner. I run my hands over it and then try to open it. Locked. I sigh and fumble around for a key. My fingers close around something. A small silver key was hidden behind a box! I turn it in the lock, preparing myself for what the contents might be. My imaginative side kicks in. Maybe it's got... something deathly. But when I lift the top, I am met with something much, much better.

There, right in front of my very eyes, are the most beautiful jewels I have ever seen.

Showing Maddie

My first instinct is to pinch myself. It has to be a dream. It just has to. So I pinch myself, hard, and squeeze my eyes shut. And then I open them, but the jewels are still as plain as day, glittering more than ever.

So they're real. Gorgeous, magnificent jewels are hidden in my uncle's attic. But why? Maybe they belonged to his wife. Or maybe he stole them. No, they belonged to his wife, I decide.

I tentatively reach my hand out and run my fingers along them delicately. They are cool and smooth. There are a whole variety; emeralds, rubies, garnets, pearls, topaz, sapphires, amethysts, even the occasional diamond. I lift them up slowly, examining them. In doing this I realize that they are far too fancy to belong to Uncle, even though he is wealthy. Hmmm...

Suddenly I hear more noise down below and decide to explore this again tonight. I lock the chest and shove it back in the corner, hiding the key where it had been. I make my way back to the trapdoor and look down the hole. There is nobody below me, but the ladder has been taken down, put away behind the cupboard again! How am I supposed to get down now? I run over to the dusty window and I eventually manage to crank it open, with much difficulty. I look down. It is a big drop and I don't want to risk it. I go back to the trapdoor. I stick my head down and peer around. I hoist myself down, my feet a foot from the ground and my hands gripping the edge of the attic floor next to the trapdoor. I let go with one hand and then the other. It makes quite a noise, and the trapdoor is still open, so I hoist up the ladder again. I run back up and put it right underneath the trapdoor, before climbing up and closing it. That was rather risky, I am not tempted to do it again. I replace the ladder and then go outside to post my letter to Molly, still thinking about the jewels. I wonder why they are in the attic, in a rusty chest instead of out in the open for everyone to see. I slip the letter in the mailbox and go back inside to find Maddie and tell her about the jewels, giving she's done with the dishes. I find her in our room – so she's finished, good – fumbling at the woven bracelet that Mum gave her ages ago like she always does when she is sad. I skip up to her. She has a solemn face and is still fumbling. "Maddie, are you alright?' I ask softly. 'Is there anything wrong?" "Oh Elizabeth, I am just remembering Dad. Do you remember how he used to be a carpenter? Oh, of course you don't. Well, I was coming out of the kitchen after having done the dishes when I noticed something familiar – it was the cabinet that I had noticed earlier. Dad's work is in the living room! That made me cry again." "I know. I still miss Dad and Mum lots." It takes me a moment to decide whether I should tell Maddie about the jewels. But in the end, I realize that Maddie is my sister and I need to tell her. So I take a deep breath and hope she believes me.

"I have intriguing news. You remember how Uncle said not to go in the attic? Well, my curiosity got the better of me when I saw a trapdoor after supper. I climbed up a ladder and made my-" Maddie cuts me off. "Oh, I'm so sorry! I dismantled that ladder! I wondered why it was there.' Catching my glance, she adds 'Sorry, keep going." "Anyway," I continued, cross at Maddie, "I climbed the ladder and made my way into the attic. There is a bit of broken glass, but that's not the important thing. There's a rusty chest in one corner and, using a key I found, I opened it. And you'll never guess what's inside this chest." "What? Old pictures of Dad? Some of Dad's things?" "Better. In front of my eyes were tons and tons of jewels, rubies, emeralds, even diamonds. What puzzles me is why they're up there instead of on display or in a box exposed down here. And as far as I know, Uncle sold his wife's possessions when she died, so why would he still have these? They're also far too expensive to have ever belonged to him."

Maddie looks enormously surprised. "How about we could go investigate tonight. You coming?"

"Why would I not? This is a mystery. And we're going to crack it." That night I shake Maddie awake. I fish out my dim flashlight Charlotte gave me for my birthday once and pull on my slippers. Maddie rubs her eyes. I shake her some more and eventually she drags herself out of bed. I cannot blame her, it is around three o'clock at night. We make our way out of the room very quietly and over to the attic trapdoor. I point at it. Maddie nods and rubs her eyes again. I carefully lift the ladder up and place it below the trapdoor. Maddie seems more awake now. I cautiously begin climbing the ladder and motion for her to follow. I reach the trapdoor and it creaks open as I push on it. It is even darker than down below and I shudder. Maddie seems to read my mind and lays her hand on my shoulder. At least I am not doing this alone. I switch on the flashlight and hoist myself onto the attic floor. Maddie follows soon after. It is barely brighter so I go back down and turn on the hall night-light. I climb back up and leave the trapdoor open a crack so we can see a bit better. I lead Maddie over to the corner where I sighted the chest. There it was, tucked in the corner, looking very untouched. "Are you ready for the sight of your life?" I whisper to Maddie. She nods eagerly in reply. I retrieve the silver key and twist it in the lock. And there they are, the magnificent jewels that I had seen the day before. Maddie gasps. I fumble with them a bit and find a beautiful sapphire necklace. Giggling, I fasten the clasp around my neck. I dance around the room like a princess. But then I realize these are not my jewels. I take the necklace off and look for more clues to why they are up here. I turn to take the chest back from Maddie, but she's staring at something that looks like an ordinary scrap of paper. Then she tears her eyes away from it and looks at me, goggling.

"Elizabeth... I think you should see this..."

She tosses the scrap of paper onto my lap and I pick it up. My eyes flash to the formal signature at the bottom – it is Prince Phillip's signature. 'Dear Princess Margaret Rose, Your sister Elizabeth is to be crowned sometime in 1953. You are to give her these jewels at her coronation. But you must keep them well-hidden until the special day. Please do not touch them, they are going to become Elizabeth's. Also, I am very sorry for the loss of your father, please take care. Thank you and see you at the coronation.

Phillip.' My mind races. So these jewels are going to belong to the queen! And someone has stolen them! I wonder why, and how they got all the way to America. Maddie glances at me curiously. I push the letter towards her and start thinking. The only possible suspect I can come up with is Uncle Henry. He is a cross, grumpy man who doesn't like kids. He is more likely to be a criminal than anything else. Come to think of it, I don't actually know what his job is. And of course the jewels are in his attic! He is a very big suspect. I am extremely excited since I have read lots of mystery novels and this mystery involves the robbery of jewels from a princess! I pull out my emergency notepad and scribble down some thoughts and our suspect, Uncle. Maddie is done reading and she says she thinks it is him too. I nod in agreement. I tell her we will discuss this tomorrow and she sighs. She must love the mystery thing as well. We clamber back over to the trapdoor, after tidying away the chest and key. I turn of the flashlight and begin descending the ladder. I get to the bottom and Maddie follows. Suddenly I hear something. I hear a groan followed by a creak and a slam of a door. "Uncle," I whisper. I push the ladder against the wall and we run back to our room, shutting the door. I am out of breath and my heart is beating awfully fast. We climb into bed and make it look like we asleep. After a few minutes I am sure he is gone. I roll over to face Maddie. "That was close," I whisper. "Awfully." She sighs. "It was amazing though. I'm certain it was Uncle who stole them." "I agree." I roll back over. "Goodnight." "Goodnight," I hear back. I shut my eyes and fall asleep.

Marissa's Boyfriend Comes

U ncle comes into our room in the morning and I have to suppress a scowl. I remember the jewels from last night – we had decided Uncle was the thief.

"Good morning, girls. I had a phone call with that woman I met last night – Marissa – and we agreed to meet for brunch today at a popular diner. She is going to bring her boyfriend, whose name is Oscar. We shall have a quick breakfast here, and then I would like you both to put on your nicest clothes and be ready by ten, all right?"

"All right," Maddie says back. Uncle smiles and leaves the room. He appears to be in a very good mood.

I turn to Maddie. "I was looking forward to reading books all day. Oh well, I suppose it'll be nice to have a nice lunch."

After a dull breakfast of porridge oats, we put on some nice clothes, read for a bit, and meet Uncle downstairs at ten, like he asked us to do. We put on our coats and follow Uncle outside.

"We're going to go to a diner, like I said. Have you girls ever been to a diner before?" Uncle asks us.

"No," Maddie replies. "The Earl never took us out for meals."

Uncle seems a little surprised by this. "Well, I'm... I'm sure you'll highly enjoy this diner. It's called Root Beer Fizzle. You know what a root beer is, I'm assuming?"

"No, we don't," I tell him. "But we've heard of beer – isn't that for adults?"

Uncle gasps. "No? Do you at least know what soda is?"

I shake my head. "I'm afraid not."

Uncle gazes at us. "It's going to be one of the nicest things you've ever tasted. Please tell me you know what ice cream is."

Maddie nods. "Yes, we know what ice cream is, but we've never tried it."

Our guardian seems flabbergasted. "You've been brought up the wrong way. I know there was the war and everything, but no ice cream? Ever? This is awful. Come on, let's get in the car. I don't want to be late for Marissa."

Maddie and I follow Uncle to the automobile. We climb into the back, and he starts up the engine. As we sputter along the road, I think about what Uncle had said. Had we really been missing out on something the whole time we lived with the Earl? Ice cream always sounded like a dream, but it wasn't very long ago that we had ration booklets, and even after the war was over, we still had a small amount of sugar. Had ice cream really been around the whole time, but the Earl never let us have any? I never knew he was so cruel. He always told us that ice cream had been banned since the war started so we couldn't eat any, and, since he told us that from a very young age, we grew up believing that. So he lied to us. Fabulous.

We pull up outside a small, blue building with faded, painted red letters on it that spell Root Beer Fizzle in an arc over the equally-as-red door. There was a large painted picture of ice cream in a bowl, with something that looked like peeled... bananas. There was a cherry on top of the ice cream painting, and it was gleaming in the sun. The roof was slightly lopsided.

Uncle pushes open the door. A small bell tinkles to announce our arrival to the customers in the diner. A few people glance at us as we come in, but I'm not looking at the people. I'm looking at the diner.

It was probably the most red-and-blue place I've ever seen. There was a counter, where people sat, devouring ice cream, and some drinking fizzy things out of cups. Were those root beers? The stools they sat on had red cushions on them, and they were round. All of the waiters and waitresses were standing behind the counter, bustling about, taking orders, preparing ice cream. On the wall behind the counter, there was the name Root Beer Fizzle painted again, and there was a large menu pasted to the wall. There were also posters tacked to the wall all around the shop, some of them bearing a woman with short, blonde hair. "Marilyn Monroe" was written on the posters in big, bold letters. Other, newer posters showed a young man, and "Elvis Presley" was written on those ones. Some other posters had more pictures of ice cream on them, advertising different kinds of soda, and showing pictures of happy children licking cones and drinking drinks.

The floor was tiled in black and white. The walls were bright blue. There were comfortable-looking red booths all around the shop, where more people were sitting, tucking into hamburgers. There were shelves pushed against the side, with sweets of all kinds stacked upon them. My eyes practically fall out of my head as I gaze at the place in awe. Maddie is gaping too. But Uncle doesn't even blink. He walks right over to one of the booths, where the lady from last night is sitting. She's sitting with a man. They haven't ordered yet, presumably out of courtesy for us. I smile at them.

Marissa stands up. "Hello, Henry!" She looks at us. "Oh, hello, children," she says, smiling a bit less. Maybe she's not a fan of children either. But she seems quite nice, nonetheless.

"This is Oscar, my boyfriend. Oscar, these are the people I met last night. Henry gave me his phone number so we could meet up again, which was very nice of him." I seem to be the only one who notices that her tone is quite sarcastic.

Oscar holds out his hand, and Uncle shakes it. "Pleasure to meet you," he says, and smiles at Oscar.

Oscar is a rather handsome young man, who looks about the same age as Marissa. He has blonde hair, which is equally as blonde as Marissa's. He's wearing a blue, button-up shirt, and some plaid shorts. He grins a rather toothy grin at us, and goes back to his menu. Marissa smiles again, and sits back down.

"Here are some menus," she says, and hands them to us. "Please sit down," she adds, and gestures to the booth. Uncle sits down, and we sit down next to him. I consult my menu, which was written using a typewriter.

ROOT BEER FIZZLE

- Ice cream sundae: Bowl containing three scoops of ice cream of the flavor of your choice, with a cherry on top.

- Banana split: An ice cream sundae with two peeled bananas, drizzled in caramel sauce with a cherry on top.

Everything looks absolutely delicious. I skip down to the bottom of the menu, where the last item was written.

Fizzle's famous ROOT BEER FLOAT: Root beer with a large scoop of vanilla ice cream on top.

That settled it. I was having the root beer float. It was a perfect way to try root beer and ice cream all in one go.

A scrawny little waiter shuffled over to our table. His face was covered in pimples, he had braces, and he was scowling, staring at us with his little beady eyes. When he spoke, his voice was monotonous, and sounded unpleasant. It was like he had memorized some words and was very used to saying them over and over again.

"Good morning and welcome to Root Beer Fizzle. I'm Seth, and I'll be your waiter today. Have you decided on your meal yet?" He whipped out a little notepad, presumably to write down what we wanted.

Uncle looked around the table. "Are we all ready to order?" We all nodded and murmured 'yes'. Uncle grinned at Seth. "All right then. I'll have the bacon cheeseburger supreme, and a banana split for dessert, please. And you, girls?"

Maddie reads her menu off hurriedly. "And I'll have the... all-toppings hot dog, and an ice cream soda for dessert." She grins at the waiter a little too widely.

I pick up my menu. "I'll have the root beer float, if you please."

Uncle raises an eyebrow. "No main course?"

I jump. "Oh, yes, of course. Um..." I consult my menu, having entirely forgotten about my actual meal. "Um... can I have the kids' cheeseburger, please?" I didn't want to spoil my appetite, not before my float came.

Oscar ordered the whopping double-patty cheeseburger with extra cheese and a vanilla ice cream cone, and Marissa ordered a plain lettuce salad with something called balsamic vinaigrette, without any dessert. Maybe she was a vegetarian.

"Bacon cheeseburger, banana split, hot dog, ice cream soda, root beer float, kids' cheeseburger, double-patty cheeseburger, salad with vinaigrette. Coming right up." Seth shuffled away, scribbling on his notepad.

About ten minutes later, after Maddie and I had to watch Uncle and Oscar converse awkwardly, our food arrives. All the burgers came with something called "fries", which were little fried potato things. I pick one up, and nibble the end of it. It was delicious, so I shove it in my mouth and start gobbling the rest of them.

"Elizabeth, eat your burger. You can't just eat fries." Uncle tells me.

I swallow my mouthful of fries. "Oh, all right." I look at the burger, which was a meat patty with a slice of cheese on top, with something called ketchup squeezed inside, sandwiched between two bread buns. "How are you supposed to hold it?"

Uncle sighs and picks up his burger. "Like this," he says. Both of his hands are clasping the sides of the burger. He brings it to his mouth, and promptly takes another large bite. He chews for a bit and then swallows. "Now you try."

I pick it up, but it falls out of my hands and back onto my plate. I try again. It feels strange in my grasp, but I bring it to my mouth and chomp. It was amazing. The ketchup was my favorite part, along with the juicy meat patty, and the melting cheese complimented it excellently. I wolf it down in a matter of minutes. Smiling, Uncle turns to Maddie to help her with her hot dog, which was a long strip of meat in a long bun, covered with loads of dressings – ketchup, something called mustard, a green thing called relish, and something white called mayonnaise.

When everyone is done with their meal, the desserts start coming out. Seth places a large glass filled to the brim with a brown drink in front of me. It was bubbling, which I find slightly odd – water doesn't fizz like that – and

I notice a large scoop of what I know to be vanilla ice cream floating on top. There was a spoon in the glass, so that I could spoon up the ice cream. I carefully push the tip into the ice cream, and spoon out a little bit of it. I slowly bring it to my mouth.

It was incredible. I can't stop. I spoon up all of the ice cream, savoring the feeling of it sliding down my throat. It was wonderfully cool, plenty sweet, and just the right texture. Soon I was left with just the root beer fizzing in front of me.

Uncle looks over at me and laughs. "You know, the whole reason they put the ice cream in the soda is so that you eat it together."

I keep staring at the root beer, mesmerized by the little bubbles that were popping up and down. "Oh," I say. "Never mind. It was amazing, though. Probably the best thing I've ever eaten in my entire life."

Uncle goes back to his banana split, which was identical to the painting on the front of the building. It looked amazing, probably better than my float. I eyed the three ice cream scoops in his bowl with envy.

"Here," says Uncle, and places a thin plastic tube in my glass. "It's called a straw. You drink drinks through it, see?" He takes another straw and puts it in my drink as well. He puts his mouth on one end of the straw and I can see the drink rising into his mouth through the straw. "Mm! That's really good, you should try some." He removes his straw from my glass so I could drink. I put the straw in my mouth and slurp.

Another extremely delicious thing. The root beer was so good, and I love the fizzy feeling in my mouth. I slurped it away almost instantly, and then turned to Maddie.

"How's the ice cream soda thing?" I asked her.

Maddie looked up from her straw. "Incredible."

"What does it have in it?"

"Well..." Maddie takes another sip while thinking. "It's sort of like a soda, with ice cream mixed in, instead of just on top." She finishes it off. "That was amazing. How's yours?"

I slurp up some more root beer before answering. "The ice cream is really good, and the root beer is nice and fizzy. Was your hot dog good? I thoroughly enjoyed my burger."

Maddie nods. "It was nice."

I stand up. "Uncle, I'm going to go look around the diner, all right?"

"Yes, go ahead, Elizabeth," Uncle replies, still tucking into his ice cream.

I leave the table and start walking around the shop, looking at the posters on the walls and reading some newspaper clippings tacked up next to them. I watched Seth and the other waiters rushing around behind the counter, and I peered at the sweets, longing to buy some. Then I noticed something funny in the corner – some sort of colorful box thing, with a rounded top. Music was coming out of it.

I turned around and walked back to Uncle.

"What's that thing, over there? The thing emitting music?" I point to the huge music-box thing.

Uncle looked up. "Oh, that? That's a jukebox. Wonderful thing. You can play loads of songs on it, for a very small amount of money. Here, I'll show you." He leaves his ice cream and walks over to the jukebox. I follow close behind, and then I double back a bit when I remember – he's a thief. I can't trust him.

"Okay, let's see... right now, somebody's payed for song 162." He pointed to a little number labeled 'Song Playing'. "You see this booklet here?" He gestured to a booklet inside a glass case, with titles of songs listed on it. "It has all the songs on it. You change the pages like this." He pressed some arrow-shaped buttons and the pages of the booklet flipped, displaying the names of other songs. "So, if you go find song 162..." He pressed the back button two times, and then pressed his finger against the glass case. "This is called 'Wheel of Fortune'. It's by a person called Kay Starr. Here's a coin called a quarter. It will let you pay for the song you want. Choose the song, and then you can select it with the quarter, all right? When this song is over, it will play." He pointed to a keypad with numbers zero through nine listed on it. "Pay the quarter, and type in the numbers, all right? I know you probably don't know any of these songs. Just choose one whose title looks good." He returns to the table to finish his ice cream, leaving me with the jukebox.

I use the buttons to flick through the booklet. 'Here in my Heart'... 'De licado'... finally I come across a song title that intrigues me. 'Blue Tango.' Number 88. I put the coin that Uncle had given me into a slot I can see with the word COIN written above it in flashy red letters, and type in the number 88. I watch the jukebox for a few seconds, listening to 'Wheel of Fortune'. Just then, the song seems to fade away, and then it stops altogether. I peer into a little window in the circular part of the jukebox. A spinning, round disc inscribed with the song title stops spinning, and then moves up to join multiple other discs, and the disc that probably had the song 'Blue Tango' on it moves down to where the previous disc had been. I stare at it in awe. I had never seen a machine so complicated. The song starts playing. It was quite good. It didn't have any words. It has been a long time since I heard a song. Earl Grayson never used to play any music. He was too intent on making me clean every inch of his house. It would probably just have been some rotten song that wicked people like. But I remember, when I was very little, Mum used to put on the stereo, and we would listen to songs while I played with dolls. I had to leave almost all my belongings behind when we went to the orphanage. All I could bring was one suitcase, and that was filled with clothes and a single picture of Mum, Dad, Maddie and I, which was destroyed when the orphanage was bombed. I sigh as I think of what we lost in that explosion. Our belongings. A home. Many wonderful people. I had a little friend called Mary, but she was killed. So was Maddie's friend, Emma. And our friend James. We were the only ones who evaded the disaster.

I go back to my table, sipping the very last drops of my root beer float and listening to 'Blue Tango'. Once everyone was done with their treats – except, that is, Marissa, who had long since finished her salad and was sitting politely, watching everyone eat – we gathered our coats, and left the diner.

"That was amazing," I tell Maddie as we walk out.

"Incredible," she agrees. We walk to the car. Since we are a group of five, Marissa is crammed in the back with us. She asks us about the school we shall be going to when term starts. When we tell her we don't have a school booked yet she gasps and leans up to Uncle. "Where are the girls going to go for school? Have you enrolled them yet?" Marissa inquires. "Oh, school? I'd forgotten all about school!" He chuckled. "Actually, it's almost September so I suppose soon they can go. There's a school not too far away. I'll enroll them." School! I had not thought of that either! Uncle is so rich, I am sure he can get us in easily. I am so happy we get to start next week! Uncle tells us I will be in something called 'seventh grade' in a section called 'middle school'. Maddie was to be in 'tenth grade' in 'high school'. Maybe there's also 'low school', but I don't know. I ask Maddie but she doesn't know about it because they have a different way of doing it in England. But she says she loved school. I hope I do too. We return home. I still cannot believe it is home. It's so big and fancy. We walk up the stone path to the door, while Uncle and Oscar are still talking. For some reason I feel like I should not get too close to Oscar. Part of me does not like him. When we get inside, Oscar takes no notice of the house's beauty. He must have been here before. They walk to the kitchen and Uncle gets out some gin. They leave us alone, without once glancing at us. I spot a letter on the doormat and am thrilled to see Molly's address on it. I feel I should write to her again, especially since this amazing mystery has come up. I pick it up and start climbing the stairs. But Maddie stops me. "Elizabeth! Here is the piece Dad made that I told you about yesterday! It is a cabinet with multiple drawers and is tinted with gold, like Dad would do." She sniffs. "Come see." I come back down and examine the cabinet. I put down the envelope to open all the drawers and I decide that it is a truly beautiful piece. But then I feel something. It is a latch. I pull, and then a whole other drawer appears. If I were the criminal I would hide the jewels here. Maybe Uncle or whoever it is does not know about the latch. I am not planning to tell him about it. And I get the strangest feeling somebody is watching us. I then start climbing the stairs again, while Maddie goes to the bathroom. I get to our room, collapse onto my bed, and tear open the envelope. It reads:

'Dear Elizabeth, I am sad to heer you are not haveing a good time. I houever rilly like Gramps and he has a nice, cozi little cotage on Long I-land. I am having a granned time and I start fourth graid in a few days! I am so exitid. I have also made a new freind Sara who lives next door. She is ten yeers old and rilly nice. Rite soon! From Molly.' She thoroughly misspelled that but I do not care. I smile and decide to write later. I roll over to lie on my back, my arms stretched out by my sides. I am bored. I hear somebody coming up the stairs. Probably Maddie. I roll onto my front again. But then the footsteps come closer and I realize they are much too big to be Maddie's feet. It is one of the adults.

I hear the ladder being moved. I jump. Somebody was going into the attic! But who? Slowly, I get up off my bed. I tiptoe silently to the open doorway and stick my head out. But the person was looking in my direction! I pull my head back in and think. I only saw a glimpse, they were just disappearing into the attic. It looked a bit like... I do not know. The only thing I noticed was they had rather large eyes. Not almond shaped. Very round. I tiptoe out of my bedroom. The figure has climbed into the attic so I safely walk past and rush downstairs. I pull Maddie over into a corner and whisper to her that I saw somebody go into the attic. The door to the kitchen is now closed so I cannot see who is missing, and Uncle does not like to be disturbed. Unless the culprit is him... I casually open the door and wander into the kitchen. Nobody is there! Uncle's guests have either left or are just around the house. Maddie and I head back upstairs. The ladder is still there, but the trapdoor is closed. Hmm... About an hour later Oscar and Marissa finally leave. I do not like Oscar but I love Marissa. She is very kind. I decide to ask Uncle if Molly could come over to our house. He grumbles but agrees.

He is flipping through a magazine and looks very bad-tempered. I walk across the island to Molly's, with the address in my hand. It is in a clearing and is not nearly as fancy as Uncle's house, but is a sweet little cottage close to the bridge that leads to Manhattan Island, where we landed on the Queen Mary. I walk up to the door and knock. Molly's great-granddad answers it and recognizes me. He says hello and I ask for Molly. He turns around and calls her name. And then the beautiful little girl comes rushing down the stairs. She runs up to hug me. We stay like this for a long time, and then finally we tear apart and she cries 'Elizabeth!' I am so glad to see her and offer for her to come back with me for about an hour or two. She asks her great-gramps, who says yes, and the little girl rejoices. She says goodbye and we start walking back to Uncle's house. On the way I tell Molly all about the mystery and the figure that I saw climb into the attic. I even mention Oscar and the fact that I am starting school too, like her. She also thinks Uncle is guilty. She suggests that I should turn him into the police, but I told her we are not doing that until we have absolute proof it was really him. We eventually arrive at Uncle's and Molly gasps. 'It's... beautiful,' she whispers. 'I know,' I say, 'it was a great surprise when

I arrived.' We go inside and I introduce her to Uncle. I think he mutters 'nice to meet you' or something but I am not sure. I lead her upstairs and bring her into our room. Maddie notices us enter. She exclaims 'Oh hello, Molly! So nice to see you!' Molly smiles weakly. I think she is still a bit shy of Maddie. After all, Maddie is seven years older than her. I decide to take Molly into the attic and show her the jewels. Again, I pick up the ladder and place it under the trapdoor. I start to climb. Molly waits until I am at the top and then cautiously follows. I enter and wander over to the place where the chest is. But I gasp. It is gone! 'Molly! The jewels are gone,' I cry, 'stay down there. I'm coming.' Molly stops climbing and starts getting down. I follow. We dismantle the ladder and then stop to think. After a while I finally come up with something. 'Yesterday I was examining my father's cabinet, which happens to be in this house. I found a secret compartment in it and I felt like someone was watching us. Let us check there.' We rush downstairs. We pass Uncle's room, and luckily he is in it. Not looking up from his magazine, he calls to us to stop running. I roll my eyes. We get to the cabinet. I stop. Molly stops behind me. I carefully open the middle drawer. I feel the latch again and pull. Sure enough, crammed into the small amount of space, was the chest! I yank it out. The key is not there! I think. It might still be in the attic. 'Moll, the key is still in the attic. Can you go get it? It's behind a box in the left corner of the room, and it's silver. Come back quickly.' The girl runs off. I stay there, waiting. In the meantime I continue to examine Dad's cabinet. It is tinted with gold, like Maddie had said. There are no more secret compartments in it. I sit down on a sofa nearby. A few minutes later Molly comes rushing back, clutching the key in her hand. I give her a quick hug. 'Thanks. Are you ready to be amazed?' She nods eagerly. I twist the key in the lock. The top swings open and, like Maddie and I had done previously, Molly gasps. I hand her the letter so she can read it. When she is done she says: 'Wow. So they really were supposed to belong to the new queen.' I nod, not really paying attention. I have spotted another problem. The sapphire necklace that I had been admiring the previous night was missing.

I replace the jewels in the cabinet and the key in the attic for security, in case the thief noticed it was misplaced. Then I tell Molly to leave, which makes her sad. I feel bad, hug her, and tell her that I would write her and we would see each other soon. When she is gone I go upstairs to think.

Middle School and Josie

A week later it is the day before Maddie and I start school. I am in the bathroom, brushing my teeth, nervous.

"What you fink ich gonna be wike?" I ask with a toothbrush in my mouth. Maddie looks at me with a questioning look. I take out the toothbrush and spit out the paste. I repeat myself:"What do you think it's going to be like?""Well, I'm sorry Elizabeth, I really don't know. They have a different school system here. And I only went until I was seven."We walk back to our room. I start climbing into bed. "I wish you or Molly were going to be there." I sigh. Molly was in elementary and Maddie was in high school, and I was in middle school, right in between. I was not going with either of them."I know. Me too." I clutch Mr. Bearface close to me. Switching off the lamp, I whisper "Goodnight.""Goodnight. And good luck, Elizabeth. I love you.""Love you too." I shut my eyes. And sleep.The next day Uncle wakes us up very early. At first, I yawn and then roll over to face the window. The sun is barely up. I feel someone shaking me. It is Maddie. I finally drag myself out of bed. I rub my eyes and stretch. I glance at the clock and gasp. No wonder I am tired. The clock says 6:57! It is seven o'clock! Since we moved here, I had become accustomed to sleeping in until nine o'clock every morning."What time does school start?" I ask

Uncle."Eight. Eight-thirty for Maddie. They're both far away and I was sure you two would mess about. Maybe Monday we can try waking up at seven fifteen. But only if you show me you can be fast."I rush to the bathroom to wash my face. If he was offering fifteen minutes more sleep next week, I wanted to show him I did not mess around. I have never slept more than six hours at night since I lived with the Earl. I proceed to brush my teeth and my hair. I yank the brush through the knots and then tie it into a high bunch (Maddie taught me how to do one. It's called a "ponytail" here, and a bunch in England, which makes more sense.).I hurry back to our room. Maddie is dressed and takes her turn in the bathroom. I pull out my nice blue dress and slip it on. I then slide on my black flats. Maddie leaves the bathroom and walks down the hall. I hear her going downstairs. I straighten out the sheets on my bed, giving Mr. Bearface a kiss before putting him down again."Wish me luck," I whisper into his furry face."Elizabeth! Come on! We're leaving!" Maddie calls up. I come running. Uncle opens the door and we're outside.We climb into Uncle's - I mean our car. I stare out the window. "I hope I make friends," I say to nobody in particular."Me too," I hear Maddie say back. "Don't worry. Everything will be fine, I'm sure.""Easy for you to say," I mutter, "you went to school until you were seven. You know how it works.""I know. I wish I could be there for you. But I'm much older than you. I'm in a different school."I am silent. We pass trees and houses. Trees and houses. Trees...The next thing I know Maddie is shaking me again."Elizabeth," she whispers, "we're here."I must have fallen asleep, I was so tired! I pull myself out of the car. Uncle thrusts me something called a backpack."Sling it over your shoulders," he calls to me, "it's for carrying your books."I take a strap and pull it over my head sideways. It feels and probably looks funny."No, not like that." Maddie laughs and comes over to adjust me. "Like that." It feels better and I laugh at my own mistake. Maddie gives me a hug and wishes me luck, and then she gets back in the car and shuts the door. They drive off.I sadly watch them round the corner and speed out of sight. I am alone. Turning around, I look up. In front of me is a large, gray-blue building marked "Long Island

Middle School". There are hundreds of students about my age mingling around in front of it.

I slowly walk up to the front door and push. It is chaos inside. There are kids everywhere; at their "lockers", which I think are the tall gray things with locks on the wall, at other people's lockers, in the bathroom, in rooms... everywhere. I take off my backpack and open the zipper to see if anything is inside of it. There is. Three sheets of paper are stuffed at the bottom of my bag. I look at the biggest one. "Welcome to Seventh Grade!" it says at the top in bold letters. I read on. It says: "Below is your schedule:"Underneath that was supposedly a list of where I had to be at a certain time. Right... Friday... First class was English. Second class was math. Ugh. I strongly dislike math. (Charlotte once told me never to use the word "hate'. I never have.) And so on.On the second very small piece of paper is the number 63 and the numbers 5, 15, and 33. It says that 63 was my locker number, and the other ones were the numbers for my private locker combination I need to use to open it. I assume that is why it is called a "locker". The last slip of paper is just a note from Maddie. "Good luck at school!" it reads. There is a little smiley face at the bottom. I try to smile and then shove the paper back in my bag. I wander around, finally locating locker 63. I ask a passing teacher how to use the spinning dial, and he helps me. Spin a lot to the right until you reach your first number, then do a full circle to the left until you reach your second number, and then to the right until you reach your third number, no full turn. After several tries and cries of frustration, it swings open. I am glad and I proceed to hang my backpack on the hook, but I am interrupted. The girl at locker 62 is talking to me."Hi! I'm Josephine MacMillan. Call me Josie. What's your name? Are you new?"Whoever this Josie is, she certainly is curious. Yet nice."I'm Elizabeth Murgatroyd. And yes, I am new. How old are you?""Twelve. And I love your accent! England, right?"If I am going to have to live with people gushing about my perfectly normal accent, then they are in for some teasing about their extremely odd way of pronouncing things. I roll my eyes."Mm.""Okay... so, what's your first class?"I realize my backpack is still hovering in my hands, halfway between my back and my locker. Embarrassed, I shove it in and slam the door, blushing and grinning stupidly. I am cross at myself for being such a twit. Josie is still looking at me, expecting an answer. I hesitate."English, I think. Oh, and I'm twelve too.""Great! I have English too. Do you want to sit next to me?" A bell rings. It is the bell to start class. I don't want to pull out my schedule again so I ask Josie where to go. She tells me Room 104. We walk there together."When do you turn thirteen?" I ask."July 18th. You?""June 2nd. We're almost the same age!"After talking some more, we get to Room 104, giggling about Josie's hilarious story of her baby brother eating a crayon, and sit down in two empty spots next to each other. The rather plump teacher is in the middle of talking and doesn't seem to notice us. I can barely tell what she says because she has a strong American accent. I think she says something about a review test. I groan. There is nothing to review for me since I only know the basics. She hands out a pamphlet of about three pages. I sigh and take the pencil Josie gave to me. I write my name on the top and start reading."Little House on the Prairie"What was that? A book title?"Over the summer, you should have read the book listed above."Oh no. "Here is a quick review to see if you have remembered anything: 1.Who is the author of this book? Circle your answer. (Note: These are all real authors.)A. L. M. MontgomeryB. Louisa May AlcottC. Enid BlytonD. Laura Ingells Wilder"I have no idea what to do. I have never even heard of this book.I skim all of the other questions, all about the book I hadn't read. I just circle the ones that sound most reasonable. For number one I pick C. Enid Blyton is the only one I have heard of. Although I really don't think it sounds like something she would write. The title doesn't sound like a mystery. I will not be surprised if I get the worst score in the class. I think they do it by letters here, A to F. I am probably going to get an F. Or an E. Do they have E? Then D. I truly doubt I will even get a C.Half an hour later the time is up. Students start handing in their papers. I hesitate. I am very worried about what the teacher is going to say. I pick up my paper and, very slowly, I carry it up to the front and place it on top of the pile. I breathe a sigh of relief. I am so glad to be rid of that dreadful... test-thing. The teacher says that we have fifteen minutes quiet free time while she corrects our paper.

Josie gets up and moves closer to me. "Elizabeth, I'm sorry, that must've been hard! You must be really confused!" "Yes. I am. Can you remind me of the grading system? I don't want to think I'm supposed to be really happy when I get an F." "Oh! Sure. Well... A+ is absolute perfection, it stands for amazing, A- is really great, B+ is yay-you-passed-but-it-isn't-perfect, C is uh-this-is-okay-but-next-time-try-harder, D is this-is-really-close-to-a-fail-we-are-mad, and, of course, F just means... absolute FAILURE." "I'm in deep trouble." Josie nods. "I'm sorry, Elizabeth."

Except my thief of an Uncle won't care a bit, I add to myself. Fifteen minutes later, the teacher, named Mrs. Peach as Josie tells me, calls us back to our seats. She reminds us that every time we are in here, we have to sit in this seat. I look away from Josie. To my right, there is a plump boy who is picking his nose and eating crisps at the same time. I sigh, quickly looking away. Now that is disgusting. Meanwhile, Ms. Peach starts handing out the corrected tests. She plonks mine down on my desk. "You have some work to do, Miss," she mutters as she walks past. I groan again. At the top of my page is a big, bold, looming F. I lean back in my seat and sigh. The first paper of the year and I get an F. I notice another note. "See me after class" is scrawled across the top. Next to a frowny-face. I look at the questions. I only got two right out of twenty-five. From a couple lucky guesses. I am devastated. Not only did I get an F, I now need to talk to my fat peach of a teacher about it. What will Maddie think of me? The bell rings. The class is over. People start filing out of the room. Except me. And Ms. Peach. Josie glances my way and motions for me to follow her. I shake my head no and point at Ms. Peach. She beckons me over to her desk. "Now, what went wrong, child? Did you even read the book?" "N-no, Ms. Peach, I-I'm from

England, I-I just moved here." I find myself stammering.Her expression softens. "Oh my dear, I'm so sorry! Why didn't you say so? I had no idea I would be greeting a new student! The quiz will not count." She walks over to her desk and writes something, presumably crossing out my grade. Then she comes over to my desk, tears the paper up several times, and throws it away in the bin.I breathe a huge sigh of relief. This teacher is so nice! I thank her several times.

She chuckles and says I am dismissed.I rush out of class and find Josie."The teacher threw away my test!""What?" Josie asks, confused.I realize I was making no sense."She understands that I couldn't have read the book and said the test wouldn't count. So she threw it away.""Fantastic! Come on, we'll be late for our next classes. I've got Social Studies.""I've got math. Yuck. See you later!""Bye!"I rush to my locker and pull out my schedule. 356. I am going to be so late. I practically run to the room and sit down in the only empty seat."Well, a late student."The tall, skinny teacher named Mr. Evale walks up to me and bends down."You are excused. But watch out, missy, you'll get a tardy one of these days."I shiver. I do not want to be learning math from a man named Mr. "Evil'. But at I won't fail stupidly like in English. I mean, we have the same math system, right?Wrong.Mr. Evil - I mean, Mr. Evale starts handing out what he calls easy review sheets. Great. Another "review". I might be able to squeeze by with a B. But when he plonks mine down, all my hope of it being easy sinks down to my shoes. It is a review of their money system.'Jason has 15 quarters. Amelia has 24 dimes. Who has more money? If Josh has 10 nickels more than Jason, how much money does he have?'What in the world does this mean? The only American money I had ever dealt with was that quarter for the jukebox at Root Beer Fizzle. I collapse back in my chair and sigh the largest sigh. This is the worst day ever. Time is up. I have basically just written question marks everywhere. I am definitely going to get an F.He takes them back and in the meantime we have to do difficult multiplication sheets with three-digit numbers. I was never very good at multiplication since I stopped learning when Charlotte died. She used to homeschool us. But Earl Grayson couldn't be bothered and constantly said that children should be seen and not heard.5x4 is... 19? I count on my fingers. 23? I am stuck. The teacher sees me and starts to shout. "Miss Murgatroyd! What do you think this is, kindergarten? We do not count on our fingers in middle school!" The whole class turns to look at me, giggling. I slump down in my seat.

Luckily Mr. Evale is done with the grading. He hands the papers back. My big, looming F is there for the world to see. And another frowny face.I fail History since I can't list at least ten of the presidents of the United States.I've never played "American" football, which involves a cylindrical ball that you throw around.

Filling out a sheet with all the state capitals isn't something they do in England.My day has been an absolute disaster. I meet Josie at our locker break before lunch."It's been horrible! I failed every class so far! Books, money, presidents, American sports, capitals...""That must have been awful! Hey, to cheer you up, meet me at table seven, I'll introduce you to some of my friends.""Absolutely!"I follow her to the lunchroom, which was madness. Tons of noise and mess. It wasn't the kind of environment I was hoping to eat in.She leads me to table seven, where three girls are sitting.Josie starts the introductions. Pointing to a girl with curly black hair and brown eyes, she says:"Elizabeth, this is Samantha. Sam, this is Elizabeth.""Hi," Samantha waves. She seems shy."Nice to meet you," I smile."Nice accent."Another accent comment! I mutter "thanks." Okay, I agree she was giving me a compliment.Josie continues."Elizabeth, this is Margaret. Margaret, Elizabeth."Margaret has long blond hair and blue eyes. She is very pretty."That's funny, we're like the princesses Margaret and Elizabeth in England."I am surprised. "How do you know about the princesses?""We did a section on England and the war last year. I thought it was funny since you're British, right?""Yes. It is quite funny." Why is everyone obsessed with the fact that I am British?Josie introduces me to the last girl."Elizabeth, Katherine. Kate, Elizabeth."Kate looks up at me from behind her curtain of long mousey-brown hair covering her eyes and smiles. Seems like that conversation is over. I notice something in the front pocket of my backpack that I hadn't before. A lunch in a small paper bag is crammed in one corner. I take it out. It contains a small sandwich and an apple. Written on the front is a scribbled note.'Take care.- Uncle'I smile. Maybe Uncle isn't so bad after all. No, I mustn't think that. He's a thief.

The afternoon is mediocre. I am glad when the day finally comes to an end. Uncle pulls up alone shortly after the dismissal bell rings. I jump in."Good afternoon," I greet him."Hello. How was your day?""It was okay. I failed in every subject this morning, because it was a load of American things like money and American sports and presidents, made four new friends named Josie, Samantha, Margaret, and Kate, and then did okay in the afternoon."

"Good. We are on our way to pick up your sister."Fifteen minutes later we pull up in front of a big building with a crowd of students of around Maddie's age. I squint, scanning the crowd in search of her. I finally spot her pushing through a bunch of people, hurrying towards our car. At one point a boy trips her up and she falls over. Her glasses fall off. People point and snicker. She snatches her glasses up, staggers to her feet and yanks open the door, collapsing in. "Hi," she says to me, out of breath, as we screech off."What was that all about?" I ask."Oh, you're supposed to go fast so you don't hold up pick-up. Never mind about that. How was it?""Oh, fine. I was rubbish this morning but made lots of friends."'It didn't go well for me at all. I had no clue because we did this thing called algebra and then did frac-whatsits, a form of math. I never got that far with Charlotte! I think I actually fell asleep. Everyone was mocking my accent and whispering behind my back. It was awful. I hate high-school.'So it wasn't just me who had had annoying accent comments.

"I'm sorry, Maddie. I'm sure you'll make lots of friends Monday."

"Hopefully," she mutters, turning away to stare out the window.We arrive home in due course. I rush upstairs to change out of my nice clothes. I come back down in a few hours for supper, during which I stare long and hard at Uncle, to see if he has big eyes, because the thief does. They are about medium-sized. I keep staring until Uncle says:"Stop staring, child, and eat your food. What is it? Is there something on my face?"I quickly switch my gaze back down to my plate. For once the food doesn't look very good. There are black beans, supposedly from a can, and a small portion of bread. Maybe Uncle didn't have enough money for a filling meal tonight. But I suppose I shouldn't complain. I push it around my plate with my fork, trying to make it look like I actually ate some beans, take one or two bites of bread, and then excuse myself. I rush upstairs and climb into bed, not even bothering to undress. Tomorrow is another day.

G=lsed

The Phone Call

Months pass, uneventfully. Maddie and I are still thinking about the mystery all the time and we are annoyed because we have no proof that it was Uncle. But... he's becoming nicer. School is manageable and I am getting to know my friends far better. Josie is outgoing and sporty. Margaret is very curious and loves to read. Samantha is funny and likes writing. Kate is getting less shy towards me, and is very kind and a good listener. She likes being creative.

We had a marvelous Christmas Day. The only thing Maddie and I asked for was more mysteries and other books, so Uncle bought us seven each. We went out to brunch with Oscar and Marissa and then spend the afternoon reading.

New Year's Eve we spent at home. There were fireworks around the statue of the big lady with the torch, which Uncle told me was called the 'Statue of Liberty', and we could see them in the distance a bit. Uncle made a feast and then we celebrated the coming of 1953, dancing to some music we heard outside. We went to bed very late, at about 2 o'clock in the morning.

We have a grand time with Uncle up until a very interesting Friday night in late May, 1953...

I wake up in the middle of the night, according to the clock in our room. The house is mostly dark, except for a light in the hall, and Maddie is in the bed next to me, her breathing even. It is about eleven. I hear murmuring down the hall. That's strange, there is nobody else except Uncle in this house. Who would he be talking to? I quietly slip out of bed, thinking that this was the third night in the past month where I'd gotten up in the middle of the night. I tiptoe down the hall and spot Uncle on the telephone, muttering quietly. I duck behind an open door and pray that he hasn't noticed me. I finally work up the nerve to peek out. I only catch Uncle's side of the conversation.

"Oh my God, you thought... really, I had them all along! Well, just since I got them..."

Listening.

"They're in my house!" Silence as Uncle listens again. He seems enormously excited. "When can you come see them?" More listening. "No, I won't tell them. It'll be a surprise, until you come." I wonder who he is talking to. I assume "them" is the jewels, and at the end it's Maddie and I that he's not going to tell. The biggest hypothesis I can make is that his sidekick for the crime who went out and stole the jewels is going to come see the jewels, and Uncle doesn't want to tell us because he might think we'll be excited that he's stolen jewels and it's a surprise. Why would he think two innocent children would like that? It seems an unlikely hypothesis. I listen some more: "When? Ah... the coronation. Fantastic. We'll see you then. I can't believe this is happening!" When shall they see each other? I am definitely suspicious. Uncle goes to hang up the phone. I quickly duck my head behind the door so he doesn't see me. I sneak back to my room, slowly shutting the door so it doesn't make a sound, and hop into bed, still not bothering to change. I try to think about the mystery but it is too mind-boggling for eleven fifteen at night. The last thing I remember is praying that Uncle was not a thief and that we wouldn't have to back to an orphanage. Then I was fast asleep. The next day was Saturday. I had lots more time to investigate this mysterious mystery. Of course, that was why they call them mysteries, because they are mysterious! I piece together a new plan. I was going to search Uncle's study and bedroom for the sapphire necklace I had discovered missing from the chest.

Unfortunately Uncle sticks around all day, so I don't have any time to sneak into his rooms until the evening.

At six o'clock, Uncle announces he'll be going out for about an hour. That was plenty of time for me to search. I wouldn't search very thoroughly, because it might not be Uncle committing the crime. I walk to his study and start to search in the drawers of his desk and between the large stacks of files. Nothing. I then proceed to rifle through his bedroom; under his bed, under his pillows, in the drawers in the bedside table. Still nothing. I even look in his dresser and his closet. Nothing there. Under the rug? No. I walk back to my room, discouraged. Maddie is there, reading a book. "What book is that?" I ask her. "I'm reading one of your many mystery novels, to try to solve this one. It's the "Famous Five', by Enid Blyton." "Which one? I like the tenth one best." "The second." "Mm. Hey, did you know the sapphire necklace isn't in the chest anymore?" "What?" Maddie puts down the book and turns to look at me, surprised. "Really? Did you investigate?" "A bit. I just searched Uncle's room and study. But I didn't find anything." "Oh well. This mystery is difficult. Maybe we should just leave it." She picks up the book again.

I roll my eyes. Maddie has no perseverance. Suddenly I remember some-thing.

"I heard him on the phone last night. He was talking about not telling us something and that it was supposed to be a surprise. He might think that we will actually like the fact that he stole the jewels." Maddie again puts down the book. "That's interesting. What else did he say?" "He was also saying he'd have whoever he was calling come see something he has in the house." "Hmm. Well, we have forty-five minutes until Uncle comes back. Let's keep being detectives." Maddie and I decide to walk around the back of the house. We spot the attic window, which overlooks the backyard that we are standing in. It is open, there are footsteps in the mud leading away from it, and a long vine hangs near the window. The footsteps look very old and lead back to the front of the house and stop at the front of the door. The thief must have gone inside casually after having come down from the attic. I tell Maddie to go fetch some of Uncle's shoes. From here I can see the clock in our room, in the window. Only half an hour until Uncle returns. We must be quick. Maddie returns and I take a shoe. Placing it in the footprint, I realize Uncle's feet are too big to be the feet of the person who jumped out of the attic. Maybe he had an accomplice. I plop down on the grass and sigh. This mystery is getting harder and harder. A half-hour later Maddie and I are sitting in the living room engrossed in mystery novels. The door opens and Uncle comes in. I don't look up. I'm too busy figuring out the mystery in the book before the main character does. Isn't it so irritating when you figure out things that the main character doesn't, and you have to wait for them to catch up? Especially when the author actually tells you in a separate chapter and it takes the main character ages to know about it. "Hello girls," Uncle greets us. Neither Maddie nor I answer. The cogs in my brain are turning and I can't have any disruptions. "Well! What do you want for supper?" I realize it is quite rude not to answer him so I put down my thrilling murder-mystery, to my annoyance, because I had been almost to the point of solving it. "Fish and chips maybe?" Maddie looks up. "Ooh yes, my favorite. Please?" "Well, I don't see why not! Coming right up!" Maddie and I grin and rush upstairs. I sprawl out on my bed and Maddie collapses on hers. I sigh. "Right. This mystery." 'Mm. What do we have so far?' I pull out my little notebook and scan my notes. "Okay. So, there is a big chest of jewels that WAS in the attic and it has a note in it saying to Princess Margaret Rose that she is supposed to give the jewels to the new Queen Elizabeth for her coronation, which is going to be this year, at some point. But somehow the jewels ended up all the way here in America, in Uncle's house. During Oscar and Marissa's visit, we were examining Dad's cabinet. I felt like someone was watching us. When Molly came over later that day the jewels were no longer in the attic, but in the cabinet. The key was still in the attic, though. And when I was showing the jewels to Molly, I realized that the sapphire necklace was missing from the chest. I heard Uncle on the phone last night, and someone is coming round to see something and keeping it a surprise from us, which may or may not have to do with the mystery. We found footprints leading from the ground below the attic window to the front door and as we know now, Uncle is not the thief, or at least not the person who made the footprints, because his feet are too big to match them. This mystery is certainly puzzling." "Wow. That is tough." Maddie agrees.

"What do we do?"

"Live our life, I suppose. There is nothing much else to do."

I sigh. "Uncle's probably done with supper. Let's go." We race downstairs. Sure enough, Uncle is setting the table with very inviting fish and chips. I sniff and grin. They smell amazing. We sit down and I gobble it all down. I lean back in my chair and start thinking about the mystery. Why would the things be in Uncle's house if he didn't commit the crime? And maybe Uncle is involved. Maybe it was just an accomplice. Even though it is incredibly exciting, I decide to just drop this mystery. We are not getting anywhere with it. I slowly walk back upstairs and change into my pajamas. I brush my teeth and jump into bed. I switch off my lamp and pull the covers up over me. I sigh. I can't sleep. I roll around and try to get comfortable. I finally settle on a position and close my eyes. I think of a novel that I'm reading. The hero is searching the house of one person, but he suspects another person, and - suddenly it hits me. The jewels may not be here because Uncle stole them. Uncle could have been framed.

Uncle tells a Story

N ow I definitely cannot sleep. I stay up for ages trying to think of who could have committed the crime. I think back to Oscar and Marissa's visit. The person in the attic had big eyes. I don't remember anyone having big eyes. Maybe whoever did it saw that people were visiting us, which meant we were distracted by them, and decided to sneak in! Maybe that was when the footprints were made! And why the ladder was still there! They must have seen us looking in the cabinet (probably through the window) and, noticing the compartment, thought that it was a good idea to hide the stolen jewels there instead of in the attic, where we could find it easily (because we already have). And they also might think that we don't know about the compartment. They might have gone upstairs by quietly entering through the front door and tried to climb the ladder to retrieve the jewels from the attic, but having seen me, rushed to climb up and, in their haste, had left the ladder there. They probably jumped out the window with the jewels, accidentally leaving the key in the attic in haste, and made their escape, swinging down some ivy. Then they must have run to the door and quietly re-entered the house unnoticed. I think I do recall hearing a door shut. The person could've then put it in the cabinet using the secret latch! And the person must have taken the sapphire necklace with them for some reason! What a genius hypothesis of mine! But then what was Uncle's phone call all about? It was certainly suspicious... After writing all this down in my notebook I decide that it is too late to think about all of this more so I try again to fall asleep. I finally manage to drift off eventually.

The next morning I wake up very late. I find Maddie downstairs eating a bowl of porridge. Uncle isn't there so I inform her on all my new suspicions and hypotheses. She gasps.

"Wow. That could really be true. Good job figuring that one out. But then who could it be? I feel awful now for being rude to Uncle. He's actually quite nice."

"We mustn't completely believe that Uncle didn't do it, because there's still that mysterious phone call that he made, remember? And him meeting someone," I remind her.

"Well, maybe the phone call was just an ordinary phone call and he wants to meet a co-worker from another country or something. Ever think of that?"

"Why would he want to meet a co-worker at his house?"

"Maybe it was a friend of his from out of town or something."

"But there was this whole thing about Uncle having something. Your hypothesis has nothing about having something in it. Nor does it have a surprise in it!"

"I suppose you are right. But it is still very difficult to figure this out. You know what? I think we should cease the casework. After all, the only proof is that jewels that are supposed to be at Buckingham Palace were in Uncle's attic and then got moved to the cabinet, and some footprints which may or may not be involved. It's impossible. Uncle is mostly ruled out and we have no other suspects."

I am devastated but I know she is right. "I suppose that is true. It is getting too difficult to continue. We should carry on with our lives. I was just hoping this would end up like the Famous Five or something. I feel awful that the coronation is soon and Princess Margaret Rose has nothing to give her sister."

"Good. I am sad also but it is risky to be working on this sort of thing. We are only children after all."

"Yet children should get more respect around here! I wish we could be lawful detectives instead of keeping this a secret. I dislike secrets."

"Well, that would make it less fun, because being secret detectives is really fun. Anyway, what shall we do today?" Maddie asks me.

"I don't know."

"After breakfast we could play a game."

"Like what? Uncle doesn't seem to have any games." I ask.

"I don't know. I'll go ask him. He's out in the garden."

Maddie comes back a few minutes later with Uncle. "There are some games in a cupboard under the television," he says.

"You have a television?!"

"Oh of course, I haven't ever shown you! You see this black tarp covering something over here?" We nod. He is gesturing to the mysterious box-shaped thing covered with a tarp that I have been wondering about ever since we first arrived. "Well"- Uncle lifts the tarp – "here is the television!" Underneath where the tarp used to be was a box-shaped metal thing with a dusty screen, supposedly the television. I have never seen one before and it is amazing. I had only been to the cinema with Granny once but this is far better since we can watch it anytime we want. Underneath it is the cupboard Uncle had mentioned. "And here are all the games. I have Monopoly, Clue, chess, checkers, Old Maid, and regular playing cards. There are also some toys, like my old toy soldiers and some old dolls. We can also go buy you some Barbie dolls if you would like. I heard they're a great hit."

"What are Barbie dolls?" Maddie asks.

"They're a new type of doll that Mattel just came out with. They're little plastic dressing dolls. Even I find them rather pretty."

"I don't know. Maybe we can get some other toys." I suggest.

"We'll have to see. Oh, there's one thing I haven't mentioned. My old rocking horse is in the attic! I'll go fetch it."

Uncle comes down soon with an old rocking horse. I tell Uncle that it's nice but we grew out of rocking horses long ago. Uncle looks a bit sad and takes it back upstairs, muttering something under his breath that sounds a bit like "Charlie". Who is Charlie?

"I wonder why Uncle has so many toys," Maddie asks me.

"Maybe they're just his from when he was a kid."

"But he wouldn't have dolls," Maddie persists.

"He said he thinks dolls are pretty though."

"He was saying that about Barbie dolls. The ones he has are rag dolls. And why would he be so eager to give us his rocking horse? Let's ask him." Maddie decides.

"I'll ask him." I say as Uncle gets to the bottom of the stairs.

"Hmm?" Uncle says, "What?"

"We were just wondering why you had so many toys and games."

"No reason," Uncle muttered and then quickly looked away.

"No really, why?" Maddie prods.

"It's nothing, I said! Most of them are mine from when I was young." He says, raising his voice.

"But why the dolls? And I heard you say something, like "Charlie'. Who's Charlie?"

Uncle's eyebrows twitch. He stares at us for a minute. Then he speaks.

"I...Oh, all right, I'll tell you. Years ago, up until 1948, I had a wife."

"We know that." I say.

"Yes, but I also had a son of eight years."

Maddie and I look at each other and gasp. We did not know this!

"What was his name?" Maddie asks Uncle. But I think I know the answer to that question. My suspicions are confirmed when Uncle answers.

"Charlie. Charlie Murgatroyd. Charles was his given name though."

"So the games and toys were his?"

"The soldiers used to be mine and the dolls used to belong to Caroline, my wife. And of course that rocking horse was mine too. But the rest we bought for Charlie, yes."

"And... what happened to Charlie and Caroline?"

He opens his mouth to say something but then stops. "That's enough backstories for today. Now, what would you like to play?"

"No please, Uncle Henry. Please." Maddie implores.

"Oh, if you must know. Okay." He takes a deep breath. "Caroline-driving-Charlie-home-died-in-a-terrible-car-accident," he rattles off at top speed.

Maddie looks confused. "What was that?"

Uncle is staring at his shoes now.

"Caroline was driving Charlie home from school one day, when they both died in a terrible car accident."

Maddie and I are speechless. But now that Uncle has said that, he seems willing to say more.

"I was so sad that I shut myself at home until last year. I only came out if it was truly necessary. And when I learned that my nieces were coming to live with me, I was reminded of my son so I apologize if I was rude or if I didn't seem very welcoming. I understand that it must have been difficult to deal with the death of your mother's mother, your Granny Joan, and I heard your guardian on the telephone when he called me about you and he sounded dreadful, and I am truly sorry that I did not seem like a good guardian from the start. But when you arrived I began to love you like I had Charlie. I promised myself I would change."

Maddie and I smile. "You already have," Maddie tells him. Uncle sighs good-naturedly and says "You girls really have a knack for getting information out of people. You would make good detectives." At this, Maddie and I share a grin. "Now, do you want to play these games?"

"Of course! And we're really sorry about your family, and we're really happy you adopted us because Earl Grayson was dreadful, I will never forget him." I say. Uncle smiles one more time and leaves to go into the kitchen to prepare lunch. I turn to Maddie. "Now, which one would you like to begin with?"

"How about chess?"

"Okay! Let the games begin! Ooh, I have an idea! We can keep a tally of the winners, like the Olympic Games, and then when we have played them all, whoever has won the most games gets some sort of advantage, like extra supper!"

"That sounds like a fabulous idea!" Maddie nods eagerly. "I'll go fetch a piece of paper for the scoring.'

As I wait for Maddie I unpack chess and set up the pieces. King, queen, bishops next to both of them, knights next to the bishops, and rooks on the ends. I then put the eight pawns in front. I set it up the same with the black pieces. Charlotte used to have a set so I already know how to play. It was our only game. I sit in front of the white pieces. Maddie returns with a piece of paper and a pencil. "Okay, are you ready to get utterly defeated?" she squeals. I giggle. "I don't know about that. Hand me that paper." I draw a grid with two columns, "E" at the top of the first, and "M" at the top of the other. "We are ready to begin."

Maddie beats me at chess. "Checkmate!" she yells. "Told you I'd win." I sigh, putting a tally under her name in the grid. "Let's play checkers now."

I beat her at checkers, after having learned how to play from Maddie. She says she had a set when we lived at Mum and Dad's house. I am in a silly mood so I get up and do a little victory dance. Maddie explodes with laughter. We then learn how to play Monopoly, but sadly nobody can win in Monopoly unless you play for hours and we don't have time before lunch, so we learn how to play Clue, which we both absolutely adore because you have to solve a mystery, but it makes me think about the real-life mystery that we can't solve. I am overjoyed when I win. It was Mrs.

Peacock, in the Library, with the candlestick. I am now beating Maddie, two wins to one. The race is on.

We continue by learning how to play Old Maid. Maddie gets the idea and puts the Old Maid near the top of her card deck. I pick it, to my utter surprise. We are now tied.

The only game left is the set of playing cards. We decide to play Go Fish, which we know how to play because Charlotte taught us back in England. Whoever wins is the ultimate winner of this whole Olympics-type thing. Maddie and I are both aware so we play our hardest. When I have four sets of cards and three-quarters of a set, and Maddie has four sets, I ask her for the Jack of spades to complete my set and she smiles devilishly. "Go Fish," she practically yells. I sigh. I take the card at the top of the pile and turn it over. I can't believe my eyes. The card I drew was exactly the card I needed to complete my set! The Jack of spades! I now have five sets and I let Maddie know by flashing her the four cards in my new set, along with my novel Jack of spades, with a grin on my face. Maddie gapes. "I suppose you win," she sighs. But I know she is still in good spirits. "Nice job. But don't expect to get so lucky next time." As there were lots of cards and we couldn't possibly use all of the cards in time for lunch, we had twisted the rules so the first to five sets won. And that was exactly what I had done.

"So, what's my prize for being amazing?"

Maddie laughed. "You mean getting lucky? How about I lend you my favorite book and you can have a bit of my supper tonight?"

"Sounds perfect. I like this whole Olympic-games thing. It should be a traditional thing we do sometimes. What should we call it?"

"I don't know. Something about games."

"Ooh, I have an idea! How about we call it the Murgatroyd Olympics?"

"That sounds pretty good. How about the Weekend Games?"

"Well, I suppose, but we could also do it on weeknights when we have lots of time. How about the Murgatroyd Games?"

"Hmm. I like the ideas, but we might also want to incorporate the fact that we are sisters, like... Sister Games or Sister Olympics..." Maddie is always good at naming things. She helped me name Mr. Bearface - she came up with the "-face" part.

"I like Sister Olympics best. Let's call it that!"

"Okay! Maybe we can do it again after lunch!"

After we had tidied away all the games, Uncle calls us to lunch.

"Girls! Lunchtime! I made chicken noodle soup, my treat!"

'Delicious! Coming!" Maddie shouts.

We rush into the kitchen and the attached dining room for lunch. On top of the table are three warm bowls of chicken noodle soup, perfect for a cold September day. I have never tried it before. I sit down hurriedly. I dip my spoon into the broth and blow on it gently before bringing it to my lips. It tastes wonderful. Next I try a noodle with my fork. They are also very tasty. I decide to eat it all together, what with the onions, carrots, cucumbers, and of course the lovely strips of chicken. It is a lovely, flavorful combination. I finish it up in the next few minutes and ask if I can be excused. I am engrossed in my murder-mystery and I am anticipating the ending already. Uncle says yes so I thank him for the meal and rush upstairs.

I realize that I am still wearing my pajamas so I quickly change into a navy-blue sweatshirt and a black plaid skirt. I take out my murder-mystery and start reading, but I must have read it before because I already know what the ending is going to be. Sure enough, when I finish reading, I realize that I had already read it, but a long, long time ago, probably a few years ago in England. Then I remember that Maddie promised to lend me one of her books as a reward for winning the Sister Games. I am excited because Maddie has a lot of books that I have not read, like Enid Blyton's newest series called the Five Find-Outers that she started about 5 years ago. It's apparently about a group of children about my age – plus a dog - running around trying to solve mysteries with a leader whom everybody calls Fatty – yes, Fatty – and Fatty always has marvelous ideas.

Maddie comes upstairs in a few minutes. I ask her for the book and she gives me the first one in the series, called "The Mystery of the Burnt Cottage'. I read the back and it looks interesting so I open the book and start reading. I am at the bit where the team is just meeting for the first time when Maddie asks if I want to play the Sister Olympics some more. As I had not gotten very far in my book yet I agree. We play all afternoon until supper, and Maddie gives me a bit of her meal as promised.

In bed that night I can't fall asleep because I keep thinking about the thing that is keeping me awake every night: the mystery of the stolen jewels.

Part of me really wants to go to the police about it because I know it is dangerous to be solving a mystery at the age of twelve and we have reached a dead end, but the other part of me wants to be like the Famous Five and solve it along with Maddie. I also know that if we go to the police then there is a chance of them suspecting Uncle and him getting arrested. I don't think he is a suspect anymore, and Maddie was right, the phone call could well have just been Uncle organizing a meeting at the house. But with who? Despite all my puzzling thoughts I manage to fall asleep at last.

Home Sick

When we arrive home Monday after school, I don't feel so well. My stomach hurts and I feel a bit woozy. I lie down in bed for a bit and start to feel slightly better. When it's dinnertime I don't eat anything. I go to sleep after and don't wake up until morning.

We have school again the next morning, but I am still not feeling so good. I tell Maddie and she takes my temperature. I have a fever. Maddie goes to tell Uncle and he says that I will have to stay home but he might be able to come home a bit earlier to take care of me. He and Maddie leave for work and school.

"Bye Elizabeth! Get well soon! Don't be too bored!" shouts Maddie.

"Goodbye Elizabeth. If anybody knocks at the door before two o'clock at the earliest, certainly do not answer it. Look out the window if you are not sure." Uncle warns me.

"Okay, Uncle. Thank you. Have a good day."

They leave and I get up to watch them drive away. I sigh. Maddie was wrong. I was going to get very bored very quickly.

I take out my sketchpad and start to draw a cat. Yes, I like drawing. Mostly cute animals. But when I get the cat's whiskers all wrong, I cross the cat out and frown.

I put down my sketchpad and sigh. Maybe I should write a letter to Molly.

'Dear Molly,

I am sick today so I thought I would write to you. I am sorry I haven't written since March, I have been very busy with school and things.

No developments in the mystery, sadly. Maddie things we should 'cease the casework' but I don't really agree with her for once.

Keep in touch,

Elizabeth'

I roll over. The best thing to do when you are sick is to have a sleep. I pull out Mr. Bearface, pat him, and settle under the covers, falling asleep immediately.

I am awoken by the sound of the door creaking open downstairs. I still am half asleep and have sleep dust in my eyes, so I can't read the clock very well. Maybe Uncle decided to come home early to take care of me! I wipe my eyes and look at the clock. It is only eleven. Uncle's words ring in my ears. "If anybody knocks at the door before two o'clock at the earliest, certainly do not answer it."

But it wasn't a knock. They just barged right in, presumably using the spare key under the fake rock!

Oh no. This is bad. Who could it be? A burglar? A kidnapper? The thief???

I hear them coming upstairs. Please let this be a dream, please oh please!

Or maybe Uncle just decided to come home really early giving how terribly sick I was! But Uncle would shout upstairs to let me know it was really him. And I'm not that sick.

The figure is coming upstairs. I pull the covers over my head and try to look as flat as possible. But then I get a better idea and hide under the bed.

I am scared, I am scared, I am scared, I am scared. What do I do? Jump out the window???

This is not good, and me being sick!

Oh my goodness. The figure is opening the door to my room. What if it is Maddie? Or Uncle? I pray with all my might that it is.

I look out under the crack between the floor and the sheets hanging off the bed. I see shoes. They look about the same size as the footprints we saw under the attic window!

The figure bends down. I am more than scared. Who is it? Who is it? Is it Uncle? But Uncle... he....

The person's head is covered in a black sack. With eyeholes. And a mouth hole. Big eyes... those big eyes... Uncle doesn't have big eyes. I checked. And the person is far too young.

The figure reaches their arms out towards me.

"Well, well, well. What have we here? Is this cute little girl frightened?"

Then I black out.

Trapped!

I wake up later to find that I am in the dark. I also find that my wrists are bound and my ankles are bound. And that I am gagged.

There was no doubt about it. I had come face to face with the thief! Again!

Big eyes... BIG EYES! Someone on this island has to have big eyes!

I must try to figure out where I am. The dark. The dark. A small space in the dark. I shiver. I am a bit claustrophobic.

My head brushes something. Clothes! I must be in a closet! I look up at the clothes, squinting in the bad light. They are far too big to be Maddie or I's clothes. Maybe I am in the thief's closet! Or Uncle's closet. That would be better...

I move about a bit to get comfortable and find myself sitting on a shoe. I roll off of it and squirm around to look at it. As I am bound I have to push it over with my foot to see the sole. I squint as it is dark and then I gasp. It is the same sole as the footprints under the attic window! This has to be the thief's house. It has to be. But how do I get out?

The first thing I have to do is ungag and untie myself. It is time for my mystery knowledge to kick in. I remember in one book someone has been gagged and she manages to push the handkerchief down with her tongue. I try to do it and eventually manage to get the handkerchief mostly off of my mouth onto my chin. Now it is possible for me to bite the string off of me.

I do my wrists first. I bite and bite until my teeth hurt, but I have made a dent. I pull my hands apart and the dent breaks in two. My hands are free.

Flexing my numbed wrists, I untie the handkerchief from around my chin. I then proceed to untie my ankles. I am free! I feel proud of myself for doing all of that.

The next thing that I must do is get out of this closet. I fumble for the door and try to push it open, but it is locked. I didn't even know closets could lock! I sit there, desperate, wishing I had a safety pin to pick the lock with, when I realize that I might! In my pocket. I always have so many ridiculous things crammed in my pocket. I start to take out things from my right pocket. Crumpled note paper. A tiny key that I found at recess one day at school. Hopefully, I jam the key into the lock but it doesn't twist. Obviously.

I keep looking in my pocket. An old sweet that Josie had given me. More notepaper. Half a pencil. A die. Why do I have a die? It's not like I'm going to play a game or anything. A folded sheet of stickers. Some dust. That was it for my right pocket.

Discouraged, I start looking in my left pocket. Luckily, there is just as much junk stashed in it. An American coin called a "penny'. A thumbtack. I have no idea how all these things get into my pocket. More paper. A small piece of chalk. Led from a mechanic pencil. I keep digging until my fingers close around an oval bit of metal. I pull it out. A safety pin!

I am about to shove it into the keyhole and make my escape but I stop. I remember that I was an escaping prisoner and escaping prisoners have to be quiet. It was actually almost exciting that I was a prisoner, because it meant I was in the midst of a mystery, but also terrifying. Mostly terrifying. I realize that I must have made lots of noise, what with taking everything out of my pockets and rolling about. I listen for noise. And then I hear footsteps.

I hold my breath. And I don't let it out until the footsteps are long gone. I hastily shove everything back into my pockets, except the safety pin of course, and listen very carefully. I think I am in the thief's bedroom! Suddenly I hear somebody cough, which makes me jump. The thief must be in the bedroom!

I manage to peer through the keyhole a bit but I don't see the thief on the bed. They are leaning against the wall, passing time, still wearing the sack on their head so I can't identify them. I put the pin in the lock and scrape about, until the lock gives way. I push on the door a tiny bit so I can see.

The thief goes over to the radio on the bedside table and blasts it really loud. A news story about a dog that saved the life of a baby comes on and the thief doesn't hesitate to change the station to a rock music station with a really loud electric guitar. The thief starts dancing and is facing away from the closet I am in! This is my chance to escape!

I slowly push open the door, finding that it is not the sort of door that creaks, which is good. I push it closed to make it look like I am still in there. It is still slightly open, but oh well. I tiptoe over to the bedroom door, which is open, verifying that the thief still has their back turned, and then I am in the hall. I go down the stairs and then I start to run.

I am almost to the front door when I hear running feet behind me. I was being chased! The thief had realized I had gotten out of the closet! I wonder what I am going to do when I spot the house keys. I snatch them up and run through the door, slamming it behind me. I twist the key in the front door and it locks. The thief starts pounding on the door. I have locked the thief inside! To save time, I find a drain and drop the keys down it. Poor thief. They aren't going to make it out anytime soon.

I glance at the number of the house. 2754. Our house is 2548. I am nearby, luckily. I think.

We are on Rosewood Avenue NE. Extremely near our house. Just four blocks.

I commence my walk but I realize that the thief might smash the door down so I start running again and make it home in about ten minutes.

I almost don't want to go inside. I wonder if Uncle and Maddie were worried at all, because I don't know how long I was out. I pull on the door handle, but it is locked! So they are not home yet! I dig out the spare key and open the door, and then replace the key. I rush upstairs and climb into bed, realizing that I don't feel sick at all anymore. And it is only two o'clock!

Uncle might be home soon to take care of me, so I decide to stay awake for a bit. And, for the first time, I actually stop to truly think about the predicament I had just been in.

It was really a shame that I had fainted because I would have seen what the thief was doing. Probably something with the jewels. I suddenly want to check on them, to see if any other jewelry is missing. I get out of bed and slowly walk downstairs to Dad's cabinet. Fearfully, I open the latch to the secret compartment. The chest of jewels is gone!

I rush upstairs and pull out the ladder, climbing into the attic to see if the jewels are somehow here. I look everywhere in the attic. Nothing.

The thief must have hidden them somewhere else in the house... or even taken them elsewhere! Most likely at the house that I had been in!

I sigh. The mystery had started up again. I thought about why the thief might have removed the coronation jewels from the convenient hiding place. Then I realize that the coronation was very soon. Maybe the thief wanted to keep the jewels at their house in a better hiding place. And that would be fine because when they realized the jewels were missing, the police officers would probably just search in England, not in New York!

The thief really knew what they were doing. I wish I had some sort of proof. Maybe the thief wants to sell the jewels to an unsuspecting by-stander and plant the crime on them! Yes, that was likely. The thief prob-ably wants to rid themselves of all evidence.

Then I remember that I have the address of the thief's house!!! Yes! So I can walk over to their house and retrieve the jewels, getting famous and returning them to Margaret Rose before everything is over! It could be a late coronation gift.

But how, how was I supposed to do that without the thief finding out? And they could live with multiple people, so how was I supposed to know who had done it?

That would have to be figured out. In the meantime I take out the sparkly purple notebook I am using for my case notes and write down everything that just happened with all of the details. But not mentioning how I was scared out of my mind. I also write down the address of the thief really big so I remember it, and all my hypothesis about the case and why the jewels were no longer in the house. Then I sit back in bed, smile, and drop off.

Arguments and Lots of Laughter

I wake up not long after. The clock reads 3:45. I hear noise downstairs. Familiar noise. Uncle and Maddie are home! Maddie runs upstairs and dashes into the bedroom. "Elizabeth! Do you feel better? I'm sorry it was such a boring day for you!"

Boring? We'll see about that...

"No, it's fine. I feel better, anyways. How was your day?" I say, quickly changing the subject.

"Uneventful. Let me take your temperature."

She runs out of the room to get the thermometer. She sticks it in my mouth under my tongue, which is uncomfortable because it gets jumbled with the bit attaching my tongue to my bottom jaw. After the thermometer beeps, Maddie whisks it out and squeals. "96 degrees Fahrenheit! You're all better!" I gasp. "Really?"

"Yes! Now you can come to school tomorrow. Come on, get out of bed and let's go tell Uncle!" She pulls my arm, forgetting that I might still have a bit of a cold, and drags me out of bed. We run downstairs.

"Uncle! Uncle! Elizabeth's all better," Maddie shouts.

Uncle turns around. "Fabulous! She can go to school tomorrow then," he says, repeating Maddie's words. "Now, what would you girls like for your supper? We have chicken, lamb, kale... some potatoes...'

I cut in. "Ooh, can we have chicken and mashed potatoes? You make really good mashed potatoes and I love chicken!"

"Elizabeth was sick today. I say we do it her way." Maddie agrees.

"Sounds good to me!" Uncle smiles. He turns to the kitchen. "It'll be ready in about an hour."

"Okay!" I call back.

I turn to Maddie, my smile quickly fading. "I have something really important to tell you. Really, really important."

Maddie frowns. "What is it?"

"We have to go upstairs."

"Why?"

"You'll find out."

"Is it about you-know-what?"

That's what Maddie and I call the mystery in the presence of Uncle.

"Just - come on."

This time it's me grabbing Maddie by the arm and pulling her upstairs. We arrive in our bedroom and I sit down on my bed. Maddie sits down on hers. "Tell me. Tell me now." I lean in and lower my voice. "So, when I was sick today... it wasn't really all that boring, you know..." And I launch into a detailed description of being kidnapped, even how I was scared out of my mind. I also tell Maddie the thief's address, and how I locked them in so they wouldn't chase me. And how the jewels are now gone.

But as I tell her this I realize that not many houses have only one way of exiting. The thief would have escaped by now, and maybe even found the key. Even all the way down a drain.

Maddie slowly nods as I tell her what happened. When I'm done I look at Maddie expectantly for a reaction. She doesn't say anything for a bit and then she says "Wow. And there I was thinking that it had been a boring day for you." She's fumbling with her bracelet again. She must be sad.

At first I don't realize what she's getting at, but then I realize she was sad that I had been kidnapped and not her. What a stupid thing to be sad about, I thought to myself. Being kidnapped really isn't that fun. But it was true, I was always the one advancing in this mystery, I always got to be caught up in the exciting bits. I was the one who overheard Uncle's mysterious phone call, I was the one who was sick and got kidnapped. I was the one who discovered the jewels, I was the one who noticed that the sapphire necklace was missing, and that the jewels were gone. It was about time that Maddie got to do something to help solve the mystery. I seemed to be always in the right place at the right time. Maddie hadn't made any important discoveries.

"That's okay, Maddie. You know, typical day in the life of Elizabeth Murgatroyd: Getting a fever, being kidnapped... nothing special." I smiled, trying to cheer her up.

She sighs. "Well, it looks like we've gotten unstuck, anyway. But I want to go to get the jewels back and prove the thief guilty."

"Of course. Every junior detective needs a hand every once in a while." I smile again. Maddie rolls her eyes and frowns. "Not with you. I'm older than you, I'm the one who should be solving it."

What? I look at her hard into her eyes. "What do you mean, Maddie? We're solving it together."

"But Elizabeth, I'm sixteen. Nearly seventeen. I'm an adult, practically. I should do it. I'm the responsible one."

I turn on her, my cheeks reddening considerably. "Are you saying that I'm irresponsible?"

Maddie looks at me. "Well, actually, yes, Elizabeth. You're not exactly the one to think things through."

I'm shouting now. "I'm the one who found the jewels! I'm the one who heard the phone call! I'm the one who was in the thief's house! Being kidnapped isn't just a whole load of fun, it's scary! You think being kidnapped is just a bit of a laugh, don't you? An exciting thing, like in the Famous Five! I FOUND THE JEWELS! If it weren't for me, we wouldn't be DOING THIS!'

My face is twisted into a look of pure anger. Maddie looks surprised, almost frightened. We look at each other for a bit, and then my anger fades. "I'm sorry, Maddie. I understand why you want to do it yourself. But I did find them, and I think it would be best if we did it together."

"Together," Maddie repeats, almost wistfully. "Together."

"Together." I say.

"We're in this together." Maddie confirms.

"Let's stop saying the word 'together', now."

"Okay!" Maddie and I sit there looking at each other, and then we fall back on our beds, ending the argument with laughter. Which is always a good way to end a row.

We sit up again. "I think that settles it. I'm sorry I was selfish," Maddie apologizes.

"Yes, and I'm sorry I shouted, but we're both solving the mystery. It's not Elizabeth Murgatroyd solving it or Madeleine Murgatroyd solving it. It's the Murgatroyd sisters solving it."

"Yes. That's that. Do you think we have time for another round of the Sister Olympics before supper?"

"I would think so," I agree.

We race downstairs, so fast that I trip over the last step and fall flat on my face at the bottom, my slightly curly brown hair tumbling over my head so that when I stand up I look like I have a lion's mane. I rake my fingers through it and it sweeps back. It hurt, but it was funny. Maddie and I are in a mood where everything is about ten times funnier than normal, so we laugh terribly hard all over again. Finally Maddie walks over to the cabinet under the television and starts to pull out games, her cheeks red from laughing so hard. But we are too late, we spent too much time arguing.

"Girls, suppertime! Chicken and mashed potatoes, fresh out of the oven!"

"OOH!" I shout, running to the kitchen like an eight-year-old would when the word "sweets" came to their ears.

Maddie follows me, but she walks. I suppose when you're sixteen, you're officially not a kid anymore. That sounds sad. I want to stay twelve forever.

Large, steaming plates with mountains of mashed potatoes and crispy-skinned chicken legs, covered in gravy, sit in front of three chairs. Not to mention the Caesar salad in a bowl in the middle of a table, and salad plates next to the main courses. I question the salad bowl. "Because you need some vegetables," Uncle states solemnly. I roll my eyes, and then I run to take my seat. Uncle and Maddie carefully sit down. What is she, eighty?

"May I start?" I ask, practically bouncing up and down in my chair.

"Yes you may, you firecracker." Uncle chuckles.

I lift up my fork and dig into my meal, the warm, creamy potatoes soothing my throat, which still hurts slightly, especially after all the laughing. After those are gone I pick up my knife and scrape off bits of chicken until it's almost gone, then I lift it up tentatively and sink my teeth in, the meat too got to stop eating just for manners.

When I am all nice and full and all that remains on my plate is just a bare chicken bone, I ask to be excused. But Uncle insists that I take some salad. I protest that I am full, but he puts some on my salad plate and I have to eat it. It is actually all right. I finish it, and then I am truly very full, so Uncle lets me get up. I run upstairs to continue reading the adventures of Fatty and the Five Find-Outers, grinning ear to ear.

Oscar and Marissa Again

The next morning, Wednesday, we go to school as normal. I feel fine, except I have a mild headache towards lunchtime. But I can't focus at all during class, because I'm thinking about how to sneak in to the thief's house, with Maddie, ensuring that the thief would not be home.

But then an announcement comes over the loudspeakers, announcing that we have Monday off because of teacher in-services!!! Which means that Uncle can go to work and Maddie and I can run off to the thief's house! But... then I remember that Maddie might not be off. Well, she can pretend she's sick or something and skip school.

I manage to focus in my last class of the day, joy rushing through me. We were going to solve the mystery! And the twit that decided to steal from Buckingham Palace would go to jail! Possibly even the death penalty!

All the excitement doesn't give me time to think about how we were going to find the jewels, but it finally crosses my mind in the car on the way home.

It really was going to be a difficult task. How would we get in the house? How would we find it? It could be anywhere in the large house that I had been imprisoned in. And there was no guarantee that no one would be home. There could be a baby, and a stay-at-home parent to look after it.

Maybe it's a married couple and one of them stays at home to work. And the key might still be down the drain. How, oh how were we going to be so lucky as to manage to open the door, find the jewels, and leave without any difficulties? That never happened in Enid Blyton. There was always something bad that happened at the very end.

When we get home, I tell Maddie I have Monday off and she gasps, saying that she does too! The middle school and high school have coordinated days off. We both know what that means and get really excited. But then I bring up all that I was worrying about, and she says she was worrying about it too.

The rest of the week passes awfully slowly, and Maddie and I can both barely wait for Monday. But have to wait Thursday, Friday, Saturday, and Sunday before we can take action.

On Saturday morning, Maddie and I are in our room reading when Uncle gently raps on the door. "Girls? Oscar and Marissa have invited us over to their house to have lunch with them today, and I said we'd go. We leave at twelve-thirty. Are you wearing what you'd like to be wearing?"

Maddie and I look at each other. "No," I say. "We'll get changed."

"Okay then. We leave in" – he glances at the clock – "half an hour." Uncle shuts the door and leaves us to it. I turn to Maddie. "Why do we have to go to Oscar and Marissa's?" I whine.

"I know," says Maddie, "Oscar's really annoying."

"Marissa's nice, though."

"Mm. Anyways, what are you going to wear?"

"My navy blue jumper and my plaid skirt. I wish I had a poodle skirt. There's a mean girl Clarissa at school has loads. Apparently they're the latest fashion."

"She sounds like a git. I think you'll look nice in your navy and plaid. You always do. Navy blue goes well with your features. And besides, it's Oscar and Marissa, so who cares how we look?"

"You have a point. Let's get dressed."

Later, in the car, I look out the window, my eyes half closed. I really don't want to go see Oscar and Marissa. I would much rather change out of my nice clothes and lie down in my bed, reading the adventures of the Five Find-Outers. I finished the first book, so Maddie lent me the second one, called 'The Mystery of the Disappearing Cat'. But here I am, in my favorite navy blue jumper and my plaid skirt, looking grumpily out the window on the way to see Uncle's friends.

As we start to drive down a road, Uncle says, "We're almost there, girls." I can't help but notice that the road we are driving along looks rather familiar. Then I see a sign saying that we're on Rosewood Avenue NE. It's the street that the thief lives on! Oscar and Marissa must live close to the thief. That's funny.

I start to doze off a bit more, not noticing that we are getting closer and closer to the thief's house. Then I look up. 2732. 2747. 2753... 2758! The thief's address! Maybe Oscar, Marissa and the thief are next-door neighbors!

But then I notice that we are stopping right outside 2758. Uncle opens the car door. There are lots of parking spaces in front of the next-door houses, so if he was going to another house, he wouldn't park in front of the thief's. Maddie and I step out, and Maddie doesn't seem to notice anything strange. Well, she hasn't been here before. Uncle leads us... to the thief's front door! I remember dashing out of that same door, my cheeks flushed, locking the thief in. Surely this isn't Oscar and Marissa's house! Maybe they happen to be friends with the thief, and the thief was just visiting them. If that was true, then it meant that this was not the thief's house after all. But surely...

Uncle turns to us. "Well, here we are. Marissa has prepared a nice picnic for us, with watermelon and sandwiches, to celebrate the coming of summer. Be polite, remember your manners, and certainly don't get off into any trouble!" After his speech, Uncle turns to the door and raps lightly. Oscar answers the door. I squint into his eyes. Nope... not very big. He didn't really have the thief's body structure either. Maybe I had been mistaken. Maybe Oscar isn't the thief. Or maybe there was an accomplice.

"Hello, Henry! So nice of you to pop round for a picnic! We thought we'd have it in the garden, or maybe on the porch. What do you think?"

Uncle smiles. "I think the garden will be fine. How about you, girls?"

Maddie nodded and smiles politely. "The garden sounds good."

I nod, dazed. "Mm-hmm." I mutter, not wishing to talk to him.

"What?" Oscar looked at me questioningly. I avoided his eyes. "Yes. Okay." I clarified.

"Fabulous." He turns his head over his shoulder. "MARISSA! Set up outside, please. Henry and his nieces are here!" He then turns again to us. "Do come in."

Uncle casts me a glance as we walked in that clearly meant "try to be friendlier or we're going home."

In the garden, Marissa is setting down plates and napkins on a checkered tarp, lying on the grass. She is really overdressed, with a big scarf, a large pair of sunglasses, and a big hat. "I apologize for my girlfriend's attire," Oscar says. "She said that she was cold." I'm not so sure. Marissa really is making a big deal of keeping herself covered up.

We sit down on the tarp. Marissa goes into the kitchen and comes out with a plate of five sandwiches with toothpicks in them. It all looks very picnic-y. She hands them out, giving one specifically to me. But I don't want to eat anything. A thief capable of theft from the queen was capable of poisoning some so-called friends. I pick it up, turn my back to everyone, and pretend I am really enjoying it, making sounds like "Mm! These sandwiches are really good! *chomp chomp* I'm devouring it!" When I'd gone on long enough, I throw it into a bush and turn around. "Excuse me, Oscar? Would you please show me to the ladies' room?"

'Of course," said Oscar. "It's down the hall and to the right.'

I get up and walk down the hall. But of course I'm not going to the bathroom at all. Somebody in this house is the thief. And I'm going to figure out who is.

I turn around. Nobody is looking in my direction. Good. I make a quick detour and dash up the stairs. Everybody is in the garden, enjoying sandwiches. Which may or may not be poisonous.

I find myself at the end of a long corridor, with various doors leading off into different rooms. What was I even doing? Finding clues, I tell myself. Finding clues. Or... the jewels.

I open the first door, and I find myself in a bedroom. The blue bed was made, with the eiderdown neatly tucked in. There was no mess on the floors, and not much on the white walls, except a simple still life of a few fruits. Nothing much is there, except a bedside table with only a lamp on it, and a chest of drawers. I open it. Empty! This must be a guest room.

It smells like paint, not like a human being. I doubt this bedroom is used much.

The next door I open lead to a messy room, with clothes on the floor and the bed unmade. There are lots of pictures on the walls, most of them of Oscar, and one of him and Marissa, who was wearing sunglasses. It is probably Oscar's bedroom. Maybe Oscar doesn't have big eyes, but he could be an accomplice. So I begin to search his bedroom. The clothes on the floor could be hiding something, but it isn't a very good hiding place, so I decide to leave the clothes for now. I am, however, interested in the closet. Things are very often hidden in closets. I begin to tiptoe around the clothes strewn across the floor, but then I hear something.

"Elizabeth is really taking a long time in the restroom. I'll go see if she's okay." Oh no! Oscar is right downstairs! When he finds out I'm not in there...

I ever-so-quietly walk towards the closet. Maybe I should hide here. But I hear something downstairs which makes me change my plans. "Elizabeth isn't there!" Then another voice. Maddie's.

"Really? Oh my God! Elizabeth? Where are you? ELIZABETH?"

Oscar again. "Wait, I hear something upstairs. I'll go see." Then footsteps.

He's coming upstairs! I have to hide!

I run out of his bedroom and down the hall. I pass an open door, leading to a very pink room. Probably Marissa's. I can't help but stop and look in her room. Maybe there was a photo of her without her sunglasses on. Quickly, I stick my head inside. On her bedside table is a picture of her and Oscar at the beach. She is wearing a bikini, and her sunglasses... are on her forehead. I gasp. Leaning into the photo, I can just about make out... Marissa's big, round eyes.

I stumble backwards. Marissa! No! It couldn't be! The footsteps are coming closer! I run loudly into Marissa's closet and shut the door behind me. The closet feels rather familiar. Then I realize that it's the closet I was tied up in on Tuesday! It had to be Marissa. It just had to be.

Oscar is at the top of the stairs. "Elizabeth? Are you up here?" He sounds anxious. Maybe Oscar isn't so bad after all. I decide to stay in here a little longer until he goes back down, because if he figures out that I was poking around in Marissa's bedroom, he would be really cross.

Oscar is in the hallway. I crouch down, my mind whirling. So it was Marissa. She was the thief. She was the one who had kidnapped me, she had tied me up and locked me in her closet. That was why she was wearing sunglasses, a scarf and a hat. To stay covered. So I wouldn't recognize her as the thief. And I thought she was nice! That must have been why she wanted to enroll Maddie and I in school! To get us out of the house. So she could hide jewels there.

Oscar is poking around in the bedrooms. "Elizabeth, are you fiddling with our things? I'd rather not have to scold you." I shiver. He was going to find me.

I was wrong. After having looked in his bedroom, he returned downstairs. "I can't find Elizabeth anywhere. I'm really sorry." He sounded really sad. I had pity on him, so I quietly opened the door to the closet and crept out of Marissa's bedroom, glancing one more time at the picture of Marissa at the beach. I tiptoed downstairs and turned up suddenly in the garden, surprising three worried faces. Marissa was not among them. She probably didn't care whatsoever.

'Elizabeth!" Maddie ran to me. "Where were you? You disappeared all of a sudden!"

I say nothing. She leads me back to the group. "Tell us where you were."

I stay silent, but they carry on looking at me. "Never mind where she went," Uncle says finally. "She's here now. It doesn't matter."

But it did matter. I had just made the most important discovery yet. All by myself. Without Maddie. She would probably be cross at me, but I had only promised to have her come along to retrieve the jewels, not to explore Marissa's bedroom.

I looked at them. Oscar and Uncle eventually sit down, but Maddie pulls me aside.

"Where were you?" she whispers fiercely. "Please tell me."

"I'll have to tell you at the house. It's too risky here."

She sighs. "Did you make another discovery about you-know-what? But why here? This isn't the thief's house!"

"But that's the thing... oh, I can't tell you here. Later. You have to wait." I look around. "Where's Marissa?"

"She went into the kitchen to get the watermelon. Why?"

"No reason." I turn back towards the group. "I'm going to have some watermelon."

Marissa returns, carrying a tray of watermelon. She is still wearing her sunglasses, scarf and hat. I glare at her, despising the figure who sashayed towards us. How dare she kidnap and imprison me? I'm sure she wants to snatch me away and lock me up, to make sure I didn't tell everything to Uncle and Maddie. Well, little does she know, it's far too late for that. I want to run up and kick her. It takes all my strength not to shout a cuss word at the top of my lungs. The evil lady!

I pretend to eat a slice of watermelon, which could also be empoisoned, and then I cross my arms and sit there, a scowl creeping onto my face. But deep down, I was really excited. We were so close to solving everything! Now if everything went to plan on Monday, we would have the jewels and Princess Elizabeth's coronation would be saved! Hopefully we would also find the sapphire necklace. I hadn't thought about that before. Marissa had probably put it in her jewelry box for herself! The wicked woman! The more I thought about it, the more I hated her.

I stood up. "Uncle, can we leave? I have a headache." I lie. I hold my hand to my head to add effect.

"Oh dear, is it bad?"

"I need to lie down." Another lie. I don't like lying, but desperate times call for desperate measures.

"I'm sorry. We'll get you home." He turns to Oscar and Marissa. "I'm sorry to have to cut this short. We'll get together this summer. Thank you so much for having us." Then to Maddie; "Maddie, finish up your watermelon. We need to leave.'

"Thank you, Uncle." I give him a smile, and then I remember that I need to pretend I have a headache. I put my hand up again and try to look pained. "It really hurts."

"We'll be home before you know it."

The Fateful Monday

At home, I tell Maddie everything. She's sad again, and fumbles with the woven bracelet. "Why do you have all the luck? I wish I had been kidnapped too, so that I already knew that it was Marissa."

"Let's not argue. I promise, we'll do it together on Monday."

Monday. It could only come so fast.

But eventually, it did. After an extraordinarily slow Sunday, the day came, minute by minute. I wake up in the morning very early. Today is the day we find the jewels, I told myself. At last.

I wake up Maddie. Her eyes flicker open. "What are you doing?" Maddie rubs her eyes and stretches. "Why are you waking me up at seven o'clock in the morning?"

"It's Monday, Madeleine Murgatroyd. Monday." I grin.

"Oh!" She sits up. "What are we waiting for?" She gets out of bed with new energy. "What are we going to tell Uncle?"

"He's at work, remember? He's coming home later. Never mind that. What's our plan for action?"

"I don't know. I thought you had the plan."

"Well, I did have some ideas..." I grin. She rolls her eyes. "Go on."

"So, of course Marissa managed to get back out of the house. I'm going to assume they had a spare key, because you were able to get through the front door, yes? So I'll bring along this magnet tied to a string"- I hold up a contraption that I had created last night-"and dangle it down the drain to fish out the keys. Then we'll be in. I suggest we start by searching Marissa's bedroom..." Maddie cuts me off. "We'll cross that bridge when we come to it, after we're in."

"Okay. Let's get dressed."

I turn to the cupboard and pull out practical clothes. I put on a pair of shorts and a long-sleeved shirt. I don't often wear trousers. But it isn't the day for skirts or dresses.

I go into the kitchen and open the pantry door. Hmm... beans, soup... I see some biscuits in the back. Reaching in, I pull them out and take one out. Mm. Chocolate. I walk to the stairs.

"Maddie!" I shout. "I found a packet of chocolate biscuits! They're really tasty!"

Maddie rockets downstairs. "I'm sure Uncle won't notice if we take them along." She giggles. "Can I have one?" I pull one out of the packet and hold it out to her. She takes it and swallows it eagerly, crumbs spraying out of her mouth. "Those are good," she says through chews. I roll my eyes good-naturedly. Oh Maddie.

After we're all set and we've eaten more biscuits, we set off. On the way, I try to remember the way to Oscar and Marissa's house. I look about but I don't see any other people, let alone children, walking along. There are a few cars, but as it's about 9, most people are at work. Uncle's still going to work today, he trusts us to take care of ourselves. Maddie is sixteen, after all. Seventeen in July.

We keep going, and then I spy the house up ahead.

"There it is!" I shout, and start to run. I hear Maddie close behind me. When I am right in front of it, I skid to a halt and eye it with pure hatred. This is the house, and inside it somewhere is the chest of jewels, for the new Queen Elizabeth.

I look down the drain that I had thrown the keys down. Sure enough, they're still floating in the murky water. I slide my magnet down the drain and swish them about, trying to get the keys to stick. Then I hear a 'clink!' and the keys are attached. I smile and carefully start lifting the keys out of the drain. Slowly, slowly, I pull the magnet through the crack... without the keys. They must have fallen off! I try again, but the keys fall off. Again. And again. And again.

Maddie is peering over my shoulder.

"Let me have a go," she says after watching me fail over and over. I hand the magnet to her and she descends the string down into the water. I hear the 'clink!' and she pulls up the magnet... with the keys on the end. She holds it up with a look on her face. "Easy," she says.

She passes it to me and I go to unlock the door, but then... I peer in the windows. The curtains are drawn. They're probably not home. I yank on the door. It's locked. I tentatively stick the keys in and twist. They don't work. I try again. No. Again. They don't work! But how could that be? They had worked on Tuesday, when I locked Marissa in.

I give them to Maddie, hoping that the keys will work for her. But they don't. They must be a fake! Maybe Marissa had retrieved the keys and dropped in fakes! Yes, I tell myself, that's it! I tell Maddie, and she nods.

Then I spy a tree, so tall that it comes close to a window. We could climb it!

I walk over to the tree and motion for Maddie to follow. But the lowest branches are too high for me to reach. I ask Maddie to give me a lift. She hoists me up and I swing my leg over the branch. Maddie is really tall, so she can get up easily. I start climbing, using the branches like rungs on a ladder. Soon I am near the window. I face it. It is a bit scary, what with the height. Heights are not my favorite. Along with ladders. And dark spaces. I lean out to the latch and reach out my shaking hand. The latch is really stuck. I yank and yank again. It creaks and gives way. I shout in triumph. The branch sways and I grip the trunk. The window is open, so I walk up the branch, gripping tight to the branch above me. I get close to the window again and lower myself down entirely on the bottom branch. I reach my hand out, then my leg. They are inside the room. I hoist myself all the way into the room and get up onto my feet. There! I look out the window. Maddie is almost inside. I give her a hand and she falls inside, onto the floor. I help her up and we smile. We're in!

"Now, the plan." I say. "We're in the..." I look around. "...bathroom. I think Marissa's bedroom is down the hall."

"Okay." Maddie shuts the window. "You lead the way."

I walk purposefully down the hall. Maddie follows me. Most of the doors are closed, except the doors to Oscar's bedroom and Marissa's bedroom. I walk in with Maddie, looking around at the pink walls. They're rather childish for a young adult. I notice the picture again and pick it up to show Maddie.

"Look, Maddie." I hand it to her. She raises an eyebrow. "So? It's Oscar and Marissa. Why is it so important?" She looks at me questioningly.

"Marissa's eyes are important. Look." She holds it closer to her face. "They're large," I say. "Just like the eyes of the person I saw climbing the ladder. Just like the eyes of the kidnapper with the sack on their head. That's why Marissa is the thief."

She studies the picture a little while longer. "Yes," she says after a while. "Her eyes are larger than you would typically find."

"Anyway. Where could the jewels be? Her bedroom would be the most likely place. And if they have an attic, I say we also look there. But the jewels were not very discreet when I first found them in the attic, so I don't think she's very good at hiding things. You take that side of the room. I'll take this side."

"Okay." She goes over and starts inspecting the chest of drawers. I have taken care in giving myself the job of looking through the closet that I was so familiar with. I walk over to it and slowly open it the door. This time, I can see in, because the door is open. I look at the shoes for absolute proof that it was Marissa who did it. Yes, this shoe is the same. It has that look about it, I know it's the right one. I go deeper into the closet, crashing around, knocking over shoes and pushing dresses off hangers. I really hope Marissa doesn't notice all of this mess... I go down on all fours, not noticing Maddie, who was shouting at me desperately.

"Elizabeth! Stop rummaging, quick!"

I keep crashing, tuning her out.

"Elizabeth! You have to stop! Really!"

I stick my head out of the closet briefly. "What is it, Maddie? I'm busy looking here."

She gestures to the window that she was staring out of. "Look!" she whispers frantically.

I roll my eyes and go over to the window. What could possibly be so interesting? But it seemed important to Maddie, so I have to take a look. For her.

But as I look outside, my eyes widen. Outside of the window, on the near deserted road, is a sleek, black car. It was pulled up in front of the very house we were hiding in. A girl is opening the door of the car, with bright pink high-heels, a fashionable poodle skirt, a black-and-white striped shirt, and a ponytail pulling back her beautiful blonde hair. And large, innocent blue eyes, almost screaming 'Who, me? You think I'm capable of theft?' Yes, it is. The very reason we are in this house at all.

Marissa.

The Reveal

I gasp. "Oh my goodness, she's here? Why? Quick, we have to hide! In the closet!" I pull her into the dreaded wardrobe and shut the door almost all the way. I hear the front door slam downstairs. The steady tap of high heels starts up the stairs and commences down the hallway. "This is bad," I whisper loudly to Maddie. "This is very, very bad. We're not going to make it out of here alive." That was an exaggeration. "Never mind. I was being over-dramatic. What I meant to say was..." I am cut off by a sharp jab in the side from Maddie. "Shut up!" She whisper-shouts. "You're doing that thing again when you're scared and you start chattering nonsense loudly, and then you get heard and it gets worse." She reminds me of a situation with the Earl – we were hiding from our work and reading and the Earl was looking for us and we could hear him threatening to do terrible things – and I started muttering and he heard me and we were punished.

I shrink down into the depths of the closet, my heart pounding in my ribcage as if it was trying to burst out. I knock over a shoe and shudder, too afraid to make a single sound. Maddie hugs her knees to her chest and gently rocks back and forth. I know she's trying to stay calm, but I know soon that the sixteen-year-old layer of maturity and responsibility is soon going to break. I myself am terrified, and can barely contain my fright.

I hear Marissa walk into her room and plop down on her bed. Peering through the crack in the door, I watch her turn on the stereo and start dancing. Suddenly, I get an idea. A really, really risky idea. But it might just work. "Maddie," I say so quietly I'm almost mouthing the words, "We should make a run for it." She looks at me, the expression on her face obscured by the darkness of the cupboard. But then she nods distinctively. I nod back and then I frown. Should we actually try to sneak out of here? With Marissa so near? But it's our only option. We have to get this done.

I push the door open ever so slowly, stopping whenever I hear the slightest creak. Marissa still has her back to us. I can hardly breathe, I'm so scared. What would Marissa do if she saw us?

The door is open enough for us to climb out. I put a toe on the plush carpet, sweat trickling down my forehead. I step onto the rug and stop to look. Marissa blares the music louder, concealing the little noise we make. We're just about out the door when the music stops suddenly and Marissa slowly turns around. My eyes almost pop out of their sockets, and I dash down the hall. She must have seen me.

I grip the wall, catching my breath. But Maddie is still in the doorway, and I see her body actually shaking. I hear Marissa's stern voice.

"Madeleine Murgatroyd? Exactly what are you doing in my house?"

Maddie, obviously with all the courage she could muster, responded.

"Um... yes, hello, I was just... wondering if... you might have seen, erm... my coat, yes, my coat. I think I left it here when we came for lunch."

I hear Marissa's voice and it's clear she's scowling, even though I can't see her face. "I don't remember you having a coat."

"W- Well, I did, and, erm, it's purple, with, erm, yellow pockets."

"Why aren't you in school?"

"We – we had a day off."

"We?" she asks sternly.

"Erm, yes, that is, me and my sister."

"Is your sister with you?"

"Erm..." she steals a glance at me and I shake my head no firmly. "No."

"How did you get in?"

"Um, I tried knocking, but no one came... and the door was unlocked, and... well, I heard music, so I came upstairs to see if you were here..."

There's a pause. I can see that Maddie has her hands clasped behind her back, and she's fidgeting in anticipation, presumably wondering what Marissa will say. The anxiety is rising, and then finally I hear Marissa again.

"Well, it's not here, so get out of my house."

Maddie's eyes widen, and I can tell she's trying to figure out how to save me. "But..."

"NOW," Marissa shouts. And her finger appears in the doorway, pointing for Maddie to leave. She hangs her head and starts down the hall in the opposite direction. The door to Marissa's room slams behind her, and the deafening music resumes. She stops and turns to face me, motioning for me to go to the bathroom, to climb back down the tree. "What about you?" I whisper as quietly as I can so that it is barely audible.

"I'll go out the front and see you down there. We'll have to get them another time."

"Okay. Oh, and... thank you for saving me." I give her a quick smile before turning towards the bathroom.

As I walk down towards the bathroom, I become disappointed. And there I was thinking we were going to find the jewels! I gently push open the bathroom door and start slowly lifting the window. I grasp the tree just as I see Maddie come out the door. I wave, and then I crawl out along the tree branch again. But just as I turn around to close the window, I notice something different about one of the floorboards in the bathroom. It is slightly crooked, almost as if it has been moved. I could just be imagining it, of course, but I decide to go back and see. It is the last chance I have to find something out about the mystery before Marissa discovers me.

So I climb back up the branch and noiselessly hoist myself back down into the bathroom. I creep over to the floorboard. Yes, it is indeed crooked. I use all my strengths to pull it up, which is quite a task, and it makes rather a loud noise, but luckily the loud music coming from the bedroom is noisier. And when I finally dismantle the floorboard, I am met with a relieving sight: the chest of jewels!

I can barely contain my excitement. Eventually, I attempt to lift the top of the chest, and I am surprised to see that it is unlocked. But, to my great dismay, I find it is empty! Except for a single jewel, which I recognize to be a garnet, one of my favorite jewels. And the letter from Phillip to Margaret Rose is still there, just torn in two. Good. We need that as proof.

I rush over to the window and look down for Maddie. But she's already climbing up the tree. "Elizabeth! What are you doing? We need to leave! I saw you go back in there, but why?"

"It's the chest! It's hidden under the floorboards!"

"Really? I'm coming!"

She hurries excitedly up the tree and climbs down into the room, rushing over to me. I lift up the chest and show her. She starts jumping up and down like a little girl. "Gosh! Fabulous! We've solved the mystery!!! We're going to be famous!!!! Are the jewels all in there?"

"Well... that's the thing. It's empty! Well, except for the note, and a garne t..."

"Oh no! That must mean they're hidden in the house. You know what? I think we should keep looking. We have motivation." She grins. "Come on! They have to be somewhere."

But I am not so excited. "Are you sure? Marissa's really cross with you, and I'm sure if she found us, especially me after you told her I wasn't here, she would be very, very cross... you don't want to get on the bad side of a criminal like her..."

Maddie rolls her eyes. "Come on, Elizabeth! We can find them! Just think, we can be like George... and solve mysteries..."

"Oh, all right... but if we get caught, it's your fault."

'Somewhere" is right. The jewels are somewhere. Somewhere that we hadn't looked. We spend almost an hour looking in all the rooms, all the plausible hiding places. We were ready to give up. The awful din that Marissa calls music is still booming as loud as ever, so I doubt she hears us. Maddie is leaning against the kitchen counter, I am wiping my brow. We both sigh. The jewels are nowhere.

Maddie opens another cupboard, without much confidence. I can't see what's inside it, but Maddie calls me over.

"Did you find them?" I ask her, but I doubt it.

"Unfortunately not, but I found boiled sweets!"

I walk over, and indeed there was – an incredibly large bowl of colorful boiled sweets in little clear wrappers. When we take the bowl out, the sunlight from the window shines on them and makes them look sparkly.

"I'm sure Marissa won't notice if we nick a couple." Maddie grins mischievously and takes a little yellow one at the top, wandering away to see if there were any unsearched cabinets. I look at the sweets – or 'candy', as it is known in America – rustling them with my fingers. My favorite flavor is the cherry kind, but none of those seem to be at the top, so I rummage through the bowl to find one. But suddenly I brush something that doesn't really feel like a sweet. It doesn't have the crinkly wrapper texture. I keep touching it. It is cool and smooth. Something clicks in my brain and I start digging ferociously down to look. It can't be...

I lift the cool things out. A peridot bracelet! Oh my goodness. I had found them. I had found the jewels!

"Maddie! Come quick and see what's in here!"

She rushes over and I show her the bracelet. "I bet they're all in there! I bet all the jewels are hidden in that enormous sweet bowl!" We start rummaging excitedly, the music still roaring helpfully to cover our noise. Soon we discover rubies, diamonds, amethysts, emeralds, more garnets... until the sweet bowl only contains sweets.

"I think we have everything!" Maddie says excitedly.

Yes. We did. We had solved the mystery.

Then I realize something. Something terrible.

"Erm... no, we don't. What about the sapphire necklace?"

"Uh-oh. Wait, remember how that disappeared from our house earlier than the rest of them? Maybe Marissa wants to keep it for herself!"

She's probably right. I sigh. Just when we thought everything was there...

"Of course, of course... But where would they be?"

"Let's not think about that now. Let's get all these jewels back to the chest and then try to find it."

"Okay."

We separate the jewels into two piles and then both scoop up one pile so we can carry them upstairs. I adjust my hold on the precious jewels and we tiptoe upstairs, past the room with the terrible electric-guitar music practically knocking down the door. We creep into the bathroom, the chest already out of the ground, ready for us. My eyes widen as I realize that Marissa might have gone to the bathroom while we were looking for the jewels! She might have seen the chest! I slap my hand across my forehead for being so stupid and tell Maddie my worries. But we never heard the music stop or any footsteps, so she probably just stayed in her room.

Sighing with relief, we place all the jewels back in the chest. They glisten as we close the lid one last time and push the floorboard back in. I sigh. Maddie sighs. We look at each other and laugh, and then our laughter dies away.

"Now... the sapphire necklace."

I frown. "Where could it be?"

"Like I said, she surely wants it for herself."

"Where does Marissa keep her jewelry?" But we both know the answer to that: most likely in her bedroom. And that was a problem, because Marissa was in her bedroom at that moment.

"How are we supposed to get in there? She's already told me to leave, and she doesn't even know you're here at all."

"Well, I think she saw me when she turned around; I can't run that fast."

"I know, she surprised us both."

We sit in silence for a bit. "Wait, I have it," Maddie says finally. "One of us has to go downstairs, and the other hide near her room. The person downstairs can make a noise, which will draw attention, and Marissa will leave her room to investigate. The other one can run into her room and snatch the necklace out of her jewelry drawer!'

My spirits rise. Now here is a plan! I agree with Maddie and volunteer to be the one who gets the necklace out of the drawer. After all, Maddie is good at making noise.

Maddie goes out and tiptoes down the stairs and disappears from view. I become apprehensive; without Maddie, I'm alone, and it scares me. I position myself right next to the door to Marissa's bedroom, so when Marissa opens the door, it will cover me, and she won't see me. I try to breathe steadily, but I know that if Marissa sees me, I'll be done for.

There's a loud noise downstairs as if something was crashing on the floor. I smile. Sure enough, after a moment, the music stops. Marissa opens the door slowly. All the color drains from my face. She's going to see me. I know she's going to see me.

But the open door does indeed cover me, and Marissa walks in the other direction, towards the stairs. I hope Maddie hears her footsteps, or it's not going to go so great. Run, Maddie. I try to transfer that message into her mind, but of course, that's not going to work.

Still worrying about Maddie, I wait for Marissa to get downstairs and then I creep slowly into her bedroom. I do a quick scan of the room. There's no visible box for jewelry. I hope that Marissa didn't think that we would remember all the jewels specifically, so she might not have hidden it very deep. I start opening drawers – socks, bras, knickers (some of the latter are frilly, which makes me laugh despite myself) – when I hear something downstairs.

"Madeleine! Why on earth are you still here?" I hear Marissa bark loudly.

Oh no. Maddie's in trouble. I cross my fingers for her.

"Uh... I had to go to the bathroom, and... I looked for my coat a bit, and I was going to leave..."

"I told you to leave OVER AN HOUR AGO! Do you want me to call your uncle?" She's really cross. Crosser than cross. Crosser than Earl Grayson was when I forgot to sweep the floor. And you don't want a criminal like her to be cross with you.

"No..." Maddie's voice is so small I can barely hear her. Whereas Marissa is shouting so loud it almost hurts my ears, even from upstairs.

I keep looking through the drawers while I listen. "You're going to pay for this, child. You don't know what I'm capable of." Marissa scolds. I hear her heels pacing back and forth. Then she stops and blurts "What do you know? You know something. I know you do. Your idiotic little sister must have told you something."

She must be talking about the jewels. Someone isn't very good at keeping secrets.

"W – What do you mean? What do y-you th-think I know?" Maddie stutters. The stutters sound false – she was pretending not to know what Marissa was talking about. I shiver. Is she going to confess her knowledge? Is Marissa going to hold her hostage, or something worse?

There's a pause. I think Marissa realized what she had just said. "Get out of my house now before I call the police to report trespass!"

Another pause. I continue to rummage through the drawers, finding nothing. Where, oh where could it be? Soon Marissa was going to come upstairs, after kicking Maddie out, and discover me in her room! I want to scream. Why are mysteries so challenging, not to mention exceedingly frightening, since you're dealing with criminals? I open another drawer and look through more clothes for the necklace. Nothing.

"Erm, okay. Goodbye." I hear Maddie's voice again. I hear footsteps as she walks towards the door.

'And I want to PERSONALLY see you leave and WALK DOWN THE STREET. Do you hear me? NOW!'

I jump. Maddie's going to actually leave! Would she come back? Of course she would, after she walked down the road. She's Madeleine Murgatroyd, and if I know anything about her, it's that she loves a good adventure.

"Oh, how I hate her," I hear Marissa say after the door slams. "I'll get that little twit someday, and her stupid sister too!" I get a faint reminder of the Wizard of Oz. "I'll get you, my pretty, and your little dog, too!" says the Wicked Witch of the West to Dorothy.

She's coming upstairs. I can hear her stupid high heels click on the stairs. Click, click, click... I panic. She was going to find me. I try to remember the old proverb: Keep calm and carry on. But it doesn't help in the slightest. I start to breathe heavily, my heart pounding – again. I start pacing around the room, unsure as to what I would do next. Marissa's at the top of the stairs. Things start moving in slow-motion. Quickly, I make up my mind and crawl in the closet, delicately closing the door behind me so I don't make a sound. The trustiest hiding place there is.

Of course, the first place Marissa decides to go is her bedroom. Why, Marissa? Why? She walks in... and doesn't put on the radio. I tense up. Is she on to me? I push the door open a crack and watch. It's dangerous, but I have to. I'm too tempted.

I see her climb into bed. She props the pillow up and sits up, clearly thinking about something very hard. Marissa mutters to herself as she thinks. "I could bring her back to Henry's house and tell him she was stealing jewels... no, that would never work, Henry wouldn't believe that." She's talking about me! Or Maddie... I shiver. Was she going to get back at us?

"Ah, but if I kidnapped her again, and made sure to tie her up a bit better, maybe with chains this time, then it would work... she's only twelve, she's too idiotic..."

Almost thirteen, I tell myself. Okay, she's definitely talking about me. This is proof that she saw me running out of her room. I hug my knees closer to my chest and try to roll off of the shoe that I'm sitting on (again) without making any noise.

I need to sneeze. I try with all my might to hold it back, but it slips out. Once again I feel like screaming. I must have revealed myself, the cupboard won't have muffled it.

Marissa looks at the crack in the cupboard. I feel like she's staring into my eyes.

"Yes, that would be splendid... she would never get away... she's too stupid to get away... Isn't that right, Elizabeth?"

My eyes widen. She's seen me peeking. What was she going to do to me? Something awful. I slam the cupboard door. She was talking about chains. I can't imagine what might happen. I could, of course, be exaggerating. I truly hope that I am as I hear her heels click over to the cupboard. She stops outside it. "I'm not pleased, Elizabeth. You know that."

I can barely breathe. The door swings open, and I am met with the piercing blue eyes of the thief as she stares down at me in absolute fury. She glares at me for a moment and then seizes my left arm, wrenching me out of the cupboard. I try to restrain her, but that woman is strong, and I am definitely not. "You have no idea how much trouble you're in. You'll stay here with me until I can introduce you to the real mastermind of the operation. You can guarantee lovely accommodations when you live in my house – i.e., I'll chain you up and put you in the cupboard."

The "real mastermind'? What did she mean?

Despite the knot of fear building up in me, I manage to stutter a question. My voice comes out much higher and squeakier than normal.

"Who's th-the, er, 'mastermind?'"

"Richard Grayson."

It takes me a moment to register this piece of information. The terrible, terrible Earl Grayson, my guardian for seven years, is behind the entire theft of jewels from Buckingham Palace.

At first, I don't believe her.

"Richard Grayson? You've got to be joking."

"Indeed." Her grip on my arm tightens so I cannot run. I struggle. Her hold tightens again. "It appears you know this man?" She smiles wickedly.

The knot of fear grips my vocal cords, but I manage to speak. "Y-Yes! He was my guardian in England!" I squeak, my voice still incredibly high. Now I believe her. "B-But how? Surely this c-can't be a c-coincidence..."

Marissa cackles. "Oh, you p-p-poor, st-stuttering little girl. No, of course it isn't a coincidence. I've been planning this with Richard for ages now. About three years."

I gasp. "But... how?"

She rolls her eyes. "It's obvious, isn't it? Why would he keep you around for seven years? If it were me, I would have thrown you out on the streets in an instant. Luckily, after he disposed of his wife, he was able to do so. But no, he was planning the whole time, and he specifically planted that note there, which he excellently forged, so that you would find it when you were cleaning his desk. And then he sent you here, and then we put our plan into action."

I stare at her. Charlotte hadn't written the note at all. The Earl had faked all of his anger! "W-what plan?"

She sneers. "You really are an ignoramus, aren't you? This was all Richard's idea. He used you to smuggle those jewels to America – those palace guard idiots would never be clever enough to look here – and then, the night when I came to your house for the first time, I wasn't there to 'make new friends in the neighborhood,'" she said with scorn, "I was there to get the jewels back! When I took ages in the 'loo', I took the jewels out of a secret compartment in your bags, and put them in the attic, so that if I was questioned, I could tell them to look in your house, and they would be in the attic! When the coronation grew nearer, I snuck into your house when I thought you would all be out, but unfortunately for me, you happened to have inconveniently fallen ill." She smirked. "I had to take you with me so that you wouldn't blab about 'strangers' or something pathetic like that. I knew you knew about the theft, because I saw you as you looked out of your room at me climbing into the attic to move them when I visited. And when I went to find the jewels, they had moved across the attic. It can't have been Henry. When I kidnapped you, I would have killed you, probably, because Richard said if I got my hands on you then I could get rid of you, but then you had a lucky escape," she snarled, "and then you probably nattered to Madeleine about it all, hmm?"

I nod very slightly. "W-well, you know, I found the jewels the same night I arrived. The very night you put them there, because U-Uncle told us not to go in the a-attic so I wanted to know if th-there was a reason for it. A-and then, I rushed right to tell Maddie, y-yes, and then that n-night, we snuck out of bed... a-and I showed her the j-jewels. And then sh-she f-found th-the n-note w-... with Prince Phillip's signature on it, and we... we knew. And... and when you locked me in your cupboard, I realized you had the same shoes as the footprints that led away from the window of the a-attic, and also... you have rather abnormally large eyes. That gave it a-away too."

"Well, all your ridiculous detecting was all for nothing, wasn't it?" She grins maliciously. "I have you now. I'll ring Richard immediately, he'll get on the next boat to America, and when he's dealing with you, it'll make this conversation seem like a lovely little chat between friends in comparison."

I stare at her. "But... but how did you get the jewels out of Buckingham Palace? That place is heavily guarded."

She snickers. "That's the thing – Richard is a guard. A much-respected guard. Well, all the hopelessly credulous people at the palace were convinced of his extreme loyalty. So, when they realized the jewels were missing, they obviously didn't suspect Richard at all. He stayed somewhat after-hours, and nicked the first jewels he laid his eyes on – Queen Elizabeth's coronation-present-to-be from Margaret. She had hidden them inside the palace, instead of House of Windsor, where she lives."

I had just one more question to get out of her, and then I needed to formulate an escape plan, and fast.

"How do you know Earl – er, Richard Grayson?"

She snickers again. "I thought you would have figured that one out by now, but it appears not –you're so slow in the head." She gives me a cold stare. Well, it's not like it was incredibly obvious, I think to myself. "Ever wonder what my last name was? I just told Henry that I was called Marissa, didn't I?"

I nod, wondering what she's getting at. But no, it can't possibly be...

"I'm Marissa Grayson. Richard Grayson's sister."

>&Q

Going to the Cinema

I gape at Marissa. "No. No, you can't be. You can't!"

She simpers. "But yes, we are siblings. I lived in England until very recently, but then Richard had me move here so we could put our plan into action. You're not very observant, are you? I lived just two streets away from you! I saw you working in the garden at times. I can't believe how much of a fool you are."

I am utterly speechless. Marissa just sits there, with a smug little smile on her face.

"Wait. Wait – you said that he disposed of his wife. Charlotte died of a heart attack! What are you talking about?"

Her smile widens. "Aha, another surprise revelation." She was clearly having a lot of fun. "No, her death was not at all accidental. Richard informed her of his incredible plan, and she disapproved. She thought it was outrageous, and threatened to finally divorce him, because it was an arranged marriage, you know, but Richard was having none of it. It wouldn't do to have someone who knew about the plan and was against it in the house. That night, Richard injected her with poison in her neck, in a very discreet fashion. The next day, he buried her in the yard, without any sort of funeral, wrote her name on a rock for a gravestone, planted it in the ground, and told you she had died of a heart attack. Come on, you were nine and thirteen, you think you would have questioned it?"

I can't say anything. I physically can't. My jaw drops. Marissa cackles.

"Enough said. Now, where are the chains? Basement... right... I'll just nip down there, lock you in the cupboard for safekeeping, while I'm not here?"

I nod, dazed. I did not take in any of what she just said – if I had, I would have been frantic and panicky. But what I had just seen made me much less so.

While Marissa had been revealing some of the most important bits of the case to me, and telling me that Richard Grayson had murdered Charlotte, I had seen something. Someone, to be precise.

Maddie was outside, slowly inching across another big branch of the tree, one that led almost exactly into Marissa's window. Marissa, of course, had not noticed her, or she would have probably wrenched open the window, screamed at Maddie – probably even pushed her off the branch. I shudder at the thought of that. Marissa was staring right at me, and besides, she had her back somewhat to the window.

I make eye-contact with Maddie so she knows I had seen her. She continues to slither up the branch on her stomach like a serpent and stops next to the window. Marissa is still staring at me, flouncing her skirt, and enjoying taunting me.

"I'll have to go fetch the key to the cupboard, won't I? Where did I put it again?" Marissa starts rifling through the mess in her room with one hand, the other still gripping my forearm. She's not paying attention to me anymore.

I look back out the window at Maddie. Suddenly, I am baffled. She has begun to make bizarre hand gestures – first, she points to her neck, and then she points at Marissa.

"Not over here... not over there..." Marissa is still searching frantically for the key.

Maddie continued to make the peculiar hand gestures – she pointed to her neck, and then at Marissa. Neck, Marissa. Neck, Marissa. What was she trying to communicate?

"Well, seeing as I can't find the key to the closet, I'll just have to take you down into the basement with me, I can just chain you up right away, down there. Yes, that's a good plan. It'll be a nice little adventure, won't it? Just like the ridiculous little books I saw lying around when I came to your house? You want to be just like characters in your little fictional stories, don't you? Solve sweet little mysteries, like you're so clever? You'll soon find out that not every story has a happy ending."

Neck, Marissa. Neck, Marissa.

Suddenly, I understand.

I look at Marissa's neck. Sure enough, my suspicions are confirmed.

There was a thin silver chain around her neck, tucked into her black and white striped shirt. Even though I can't see the pendant, I recognize it to be the sapphire necklace.

We had found it.

I look back at Maddie and give her a little nod, one that was too conspicuous for Marissa to notice, to tell her I understand. Then I look at Marissa, my face contorted into an expression of pure anger. It was time to get revenge.

"Actually, Marissa Grayson, that's where you're wrong."

It all happens in a matter of seconds, or so it seems. I hastily unlatch the window and Maddie jumps off from the branch, through the window, and her feet slam right into Marissa's hip as she tumbles onto the floor of her room. We all hear a crack as Marissa falls to the ground, crying out. I stand there, surprised, but Maddie is quicker to react and, unblinkingly, snatches the silver chain off from Marissa's neck. Sure enough, it is the sapphire necklace. She stuffs it in her pocket, and I, catching on, dash to the bathroom and take the chest of jewels from under the floorboards. I can hear Marissa's shouts of "You little... UGH!" and "You haven't escaped yet!" issuing from the bedroom as we run down the hall. I hear Marissa chuck her high heels to the side and stumble to her feet. I hear her wobbling down the stairs as fast as she can with a fractured hip. I watch her as Maddie pushes open the door and we take off down the road, Marissa limping behind us, barefoot, cursing.

If you had driven down Rosewood Avenue at 11:42 AM that Monday, you would have seen two teenage girls sprinting down the road, with an insane-looking fashionista bleeding all over her model clothing staggering behind them. You would probably have blinked to check if you were hallucinating, and then realized it was real, and driven off as fast as you could have. Or maybe you would have come out of your car to tend to the lady, or question the fleeing girls. But none of that did occur.

We dash towards our house at top speed, clutching the jewels. Marissa is still hobbling behind us, but far behind – her hip is very injured, thanks to Maddie's good eye and her quick thinking.

As we run, I quickly confide in Maddie all that Marissa had revealed to me.

"Marissa told me many things about the mystery," I begin. Marissa herself is too far behind to hear anything. "Clearly she thought I wouldn't live to tell the tale."

"What? What did she tell you?" Maddie asks eagerly.

"Where to begin?" And I start telling Maddie everything. That Marissa hadn't been there to 'make new friends in the neighborhood'. That she wasn't the real 'mastermind' of the operation.

Maddie gasps when I tell her the latter. "It's not just her?" she asks. "Who is it, then?"

I look over at Maddie as we jog. I observe her flushed cheeks and her lopsided glasses. Then I realize – Maddie had saved my life. If it hadn't been for her, I would have been chained up in the basement by now, and Richard Grayson would have been on a boat to America, to kill me.

Without Maddie, all would be lost.

"You're never going to believe me when I tell you," I warn her.

"Who? Who is it?"

I stare right into her emerald-green eyes.

"Earl Grayson," I say sadly, shaking my head.

"No! I won't believe it! I won't!" Maddie exclaims. "How is that possible?"

I sigh. "Do you remember, last year, when Marissa came for the first time? She said she was there to make new friends in the neighborhood. But really, all she wanted to do was take the jewels out of the secret compartment in our bags that the Earl had hidden them in. He used us to smuggle the jewels to America."

Maddie's eyes are widening at my every word. "Go on," she urges me.

I take a deep breath. It's hard to talk so much when you're running as fast as you can. "Earl Grayson is a guard at Buckingham Palace. He stayed after hours to nick the jewels. Marissa was sure he would have thrown us out of his house before if it wasn't for their plan. They're criminals, both of them. The Earl's wickedness wasn't just out of spite. It was because he was a miscreant, a terrible miscreant, and I wish we could send them both to a prison – no – a penitentiary! For life! That's what they deserve!" I shout the last bit, pumping my fist into the air.

"This is unbelievable. I would never have thought it could be the Earl! It does make sense, though, he's very wicked. That time he didn't let you eat any supper because you had dropped a fork on the floor? And when he used to duct tape our mouths?" Maddie looks pained, having to recall the days when we were both so miserable.

I stare at my feet as we continue to run for our lives. "That's not all."

"Not all? What do you mean?"

"The Earl and Marissa have a special relationship. They're not just partners in crime," I tell her.

"D'you mean... Marissa's secretly dating him and Oscar is just a scam?"

"No. It's more than that," I say woefully. "Marissa and Richard are brother and sister. The Grayson siblings." I look at Maddie, my expression lachrymose. "Her name is Marissa Grayson."

Maddie opens her mouth to react, but she's interrupted by someone. Marissa, to be exact. We had just about forgotten the limping figure failing to chase us, even though she was the main subject of our conversation.

"OI! ELIZABETH! WHAT D'YOU THINK YOU'RE DOING? YOU'RE NOT SUPPOSED TO TELL MADELEINE! I ONLY TOLD YOU BECAUSE YOU WEREN'T GOING TO LAST LONGER THAN A WEEK! COME BACK HERE, OR YOU'LL REGRET IT!" Marissa makes a rather rude hand gesture at us, which I obstinately ignore.

"Unfortunately for you, Marissa, we have the advantage here. Madeleine here" – I laughed – "managed to fracture your hip, and we have all the jewels. So sucks to be you – we're out of your grasp now." I grin, pleased with myself.

"You – little – come back – you'll pay – argh..."

Marissa's leg is bleeding rather unpleasantly now. She's panting like mad, clutching her leg, but she pursues. She looks quite scary, a dark red stain quickly spreading all over her skirt.

"We need to run faster," Maddie tells me. I nod. We both take deep breaths and pummel forwards at top speed, dashing towards our house. I don't think I've ever run this fast in my life. When we finally arrive, I fiddle with the spare key and hastily twist it in the lock. Maddie wrenches the door open and dashes inside, but before I follow, I glance at the bleeding miscreant stumbling towards our door in terrible pain, cursing at the top of her lungs. She keels over, panting, and addresses me one last time.

"I will get you, Elizabeth. You can count on that."

I grin. "No, you won't. Goodbye, Marissa Grayson. It was awful knowing you."

And I slam the door shut and lock it behind me, leaving Marissa and her bleeding leg behind.

"One more thing you must know... and you're not going to like it."

"What, because everything else was good news?" Maddie says sarcastically.

I sighed. "Really."

"Go on then, what is it?"

"Richard killed Charlotte. Because she didn't like the sound of the jewel theft." There. The worst was said.

"WHAT?" she screamed.

I put my hands up in protest. "I know! I know, Maddie. I know."

"How?"

"Poison. You know how he buried her and we never saw the body?"

"I can't believe this. I won't." Maddie said quietly.

"Believe it. Because it's true."

We both looked at the ground for a few minutes.

"Right. Where should we hide them?" Maddie asks me. I knew she was referring to the jewels, ending the conversation there.

"The attic," I say. "That would be funny."

And so we hide them in the attic. I carefully slip the sapphire necklace back into the chest along with the other jewels. "Goodbye, jewels. For now."

That afternoon, after Uncle comes home from work to find us innocently sitting on the sofa, Maddie and I are reading as usual. Uncle is reading as well, except he's not reading mystery novels – he's reading a dreadfully dull book entitled Slicing Carrots: The Complicated Art of Chopping Vegetables. I roll my eyes. He appears to be engrossed in this mundane piece of literature – if you could call it literature. I suppose you really can't.

Marissa's words from yesterday, about how I just wanted to be like my book characters, had had an impact on me. I suppose they were true in a way, but they had somewhat put me off reading last night when I was supposed to be sleeping, like I often do. But it didn't matter what Marissa said. We had won.

Uncle looks up from his carrot book. "Girls? I got you tickets to go to the cinema down the road. It begins at precisely three thirty. I don't suppose you've been to the cinema before, have you?"

I sigh. "No, we haven't, the Earl never took us." I distinctly look at Maddie while saying this. We're both thinking the same thing – we had just found out that the Earl is far crueler than we ever could have imagined.

Uncle sighs too. "I should've known. Well, you'll enjoy it. It's basically a huge television that everyone goes to see in a dark room called a theater. They'll be showing the news. You know, the news," he adds, having caught my bewildered look. "What's going on in the world, and things like that? I can't believe you don't know what a simple thing like the news is. Didn't Grayson ever read a newspaper?"

Maddie nods. "Yes, but we've never watched television, let alone a huge public one."

It sounds rather interesting. "Are you going to come with us? Or are we going alone?" I inquire.

Uncle exhales rather loudly and puts down his dull book. "No, but I wish I could. I have a load of work to do." He runs his fingers through his shaggy hair and sighs once again. Uncle recently revealed to us that he was something called an accountant, which was an incredibly boring job that involved figuring out people's financial problems, or something like that. "But I got you tickets. I thought you might want to see it, but if that's not the case..." He trails off, looking incredibly forlorn.

"No, no, of course we want to go," says Maddie, trying to comfort him. He smiles a bit and turns back to his book. "Well, that's settled then. Dress in some nice clothes, and I'll walk you over there."

"Race you upstairs!" I shout. "Ready – set – GO!" And we take off at top speed, climbing the stairs as fast as we can. Maddie arrives in the bedroom what seems like a millisecond before me.

"I win!" she squeals. We both pounce on the beds, rolling around and laughing like mad. Then I sit up, suddenly serious.

"Maddie, you know what you said about it always being me who advanced in the mystery?"

She sits up too and looks at me. "Yes, I do. Why are you bringing it up?"

"Well, earlier today – that was really clever of you, you know. Noticing the necklace, fracturing her hip... making her bleed like that... without you, I would still be there, as Marissa's helpless victim."

Maddie's staring at me, misty-eyed. "Thank you."

"Maddie, you saved my life. You know that, right?"

She takes my hands in hers and looks right into my gray eyes.

"Really?"

"Yes, Maddie, you did. She was just about to chain me up in the basement and... and make the Earl come and deal with me himself. And... and she said... what did she say again? Oh yes... she said that once the Earl was dealing with me, it would make the conversation between me and her seem like a chat between friends. Which was a heavy comparison – the conversation involved death threats and things like that." I look down at my stripy socks. "I understood your elaborate hand motions about the necklace just in time. Not to mention the fact that you noticed the bowl of boiled sweets in the first place, and you made up that story about the purple coat in an instant..." I look back at her. "You really are a detective, Maddie."

Maddie looks at me for a while in silence, still holding both my hands. I stare back down at my blue socks, blushing. Then, to my surprise, Maddie folds me into an embrace. We sit there hugging for almost two minutes. An unwanted, unexpected tear trickles down my cheek onto Maddie's cashmere top. I hastily wipe it away.

Eventually, we break away, staring into each other's eyes for some reason.

"I'm not really a detective," she tells me, "but you are. You were fabulous. You stayed strong while Marissa was threatening you," (Not really, I add to myself), "you found the chest in the bathroom, you found the jewels in the sweet bowl, you opened the window and absolutely caught Marissa by surprise, and when we were making our escape, you were the one who ran to the bathroom and took the jewels back."

I roll my eyes, blushing, breaking the serious moment.

"First of all, I could barely speak when she had me cornered, and when I did speak, I stuttered like mad. And you're the one who noticed the necklace and grabbed it off of her neck. I seriously could not have done it without you. I didn't do anything to save you, you're the one who saved me."

"Not true," Maddie says. "You distracted Marissa when she found you in the cupboard, so that I could climb back up the tree."

I raise my eyebrows, laughing. "Right," I say, "I definitely saved you in that circumstance."

Maddie is giggling now. We hug again, both laughing, more tears – tears of laughter – running down our faces.

Uncle ruins the moment by shouting upstairs. "Girls? Are you almost ready? We have to leave soon, it's a quarter past three!"

Maddie and I snap out of our reverie and dash to the closet we share, randomly pulling articles of clothing out of it.

"But really, Maddie – you fractured her hip! That's wicked! I mean, it's a serious injury... but she deserved it, the way she had treated us." I yank off my top and pull another one on.

"She really did," Maddie agrees. She laughs again. We dash back downstairs to join Uncle, who really hadn't bothered to dress nicely. He wasn't even wearing his signature tweed jacket.

"Shall we go, then?" Uncle says, smiling at us.

"Yes, let's."

We go out the door and get in the car. Uncle drives us the short distance to the cinema, called Eisenhower Cinemas, presumably after the current president of the United States, President Eisenhower (I wish a woman could be president for once. Josie says there's never been one, which is ridiculous). It is a big red building with people filing in and out of it. We get out of the car. Maddie and I stare at the building in wonder.

"Well, have fun!" Uncle says. "I'll be back to pick you up at about half past five. It's three twenty-eight now, it's just about to begin. Hurry along!" He turns back to the car and speeds away, leaving us with our tickets in front of Eisenhower Cinemas.

"Should... should we just go inside, then?" Maddie asks me.

"S'pose we should." We get in line to go into the cinema. When we get to the front of the line, a grumpy woman greets us. She reminds me vaguely of Seth, the waiter at Root Beer Fizzle.

"Welcome to Eisenhower Cinemas. May I see your tickets please?" Maddie holds out our tickets. "Thank you," the woman says. She tore the tickets in half and dropped one half in a little bin. Then she gave the other halves back to us. "Down the hall and to the right, please."

We went down the hall and to the right. There was a long hall that led into a dark room with sloping seats. A huge screen was in front of the sloping array of seats. People were sitting in the seats, looking at the screen expectantly. The screen was currently off, but I was sure it would be turned on soon.

Maddie leads the way into the row of seats. People stand up as we walk in front of them and take our seats in the middle of the theater.

"It'll start any minute," Maddie says.

And sure enough, it did. It was amazing. The screen fuzzed for a moment, and then it looked like an image of real life, but it couldn't've been there, in front of us, because Queen Elizabeth was on the screen, and Queen Elizabeth was in England, not Long Island, New York. It looked exactly like real life, except there weren't any colors. It was all in black and white.

"Wow!" I said. "This is amazing! I never thought television would be like this."

"Me neither," said Maddie.

"Uncle said that it was going to be the news," I said. "Maybe something is going on in England that they're going to tell us about."

I was right. Suddenly, a voice started talking. It came from the huge television. And it was talking about something very, very familiar.

"Jewels meant for Queen Elizabeth's coronation, to take place on June 2nd, have been stolen. They were going to be a gift from her sister, Princess Margaret Rose. The jewels were in a red chest, and Princess Margaret says there was a note from Prince Phillip inside of it. Among the jewels were amethyst bracelets, peridot rings, garnets, emeralds, and a particularly expensive sapphire necklace."

Maddie and I gasp. First of all, June 2nd was my thirteenth birthday, and apparently, it was to be the same day as the coronation.

Second of all – America knew about the jewel theft. Marissa had been wrong. America would eventually find out, and now, they had. And there was the probability that policemen would come to search houses. Would they search our house? Would Uncle be accused? Would we be allowed to explain?

The image on the screen had changed to show the chest of jewels with all the jewels that were currently in our attic. The sapphire necklace was there, in black and white like everything else.

"Elizabeth, we should go. We need to go to the police and tell them that we know where the jewels are, how they came to be in America, give them names, and tell them all the information we have. We can probably show them the jewels later."

"But..." I protested, "I want to watch the television! Isn't it amazing? And didn't we say that we were going to solve the mystery ourselves?"

"Yes... it is amazing... but this is urgent. We have to prove we've solved the mystery, and catch Marissa off guard. And we have a chance to get revenge on Richard Grayson." She smiles maliciously.

"Oh... all right then. I suppose it will be rather satisfying."

Maddie clasps my hand and leads me out of the auditorium, to the annoyance of many people, for we were rather blocking the view. I was sad to have to cut our cinema experience short, but we desperately needed to get the mystery out of the way.

The surly woman at the front desk asks – well, shouts, more like – us where we're headed. We simply dash out without saying anything, to her utter irritation.

"Where d'you think you're going?" she yells. "The show isn't over yet!"

But we run out, right down the road, to the nearest police station. It was a squat, blue building with the word "POLICE" painted in yellow on the door. Maddie and I rushed inside.

A plump policeman was sitting behind the desk, scowling.

"Excuse me?" Maddie says timidly. "Erm... we know the whereabouts of the missing jewels from Buckingham Palace."

"You do, do you?" he says, smiling to himself. Suddenly I am aware that he probably gets this every day. A pit burrows into my stomach. Would he believe us?

"Would you mind telling me exactly what the contents of the box of jewels is?" the policeman goes on.

"Just about," I pipe up. "There's a sapphire necklace, many peridot bracelets, some diamond rings... emeralds... garnets... rubies... I think there was a large amethyst ring..."

"All right," the policeman interrupts. "You could have got that from any newspaper, it's all over the news. Where exactly are these jewels?"

"They're in our attic," Maddie says.

"In your attic. Of course. Do you have any proof of this? Do you know whether these are the right jewels?"

"Yes! We do. First of all, we just saw the news, and they look identical. Second of all, there's a note in the box of jewels addressed to Margaret Rose with Prince Phillip's signature on it," Maddie tells the policeman very fast.

"Mm-hmm. So... why are they in your attic? Did you steal them?" He chuckles. Now I am convinced he doesn't believe us. We had to convince him, then. I exchange a glance with Maddie. She seems to be thinking the same thing as I am. We nod at each other.

"No, of course we didn't, or else why would we be here?" she says.

"So tell me why they are in your attic."

Maddie and I both start talking at the same time, cutting in at random moments.

"– came to our house..."

"– I went in the attic..."

"– Root Beer Fizzle..."

"– father's cabinet..."

"– sapphire necklace was missing..."

"– the silver key..."

"– my sister was kidnapped..."

"– went to their house for a picnic..."

"– they were our friends..."

"– big eyes..."

"– off school..."

"– Marissa Grayson..."

"– searched her bedroom..."

"– they were in a huge sweet bowl..."

"Hang on! HANG ON! I'm sure it took you ages to rehearse this cock-and-bull story, but I'm going to have to stop you there. Please get out of this establishment. The police department does not have the time for teenage shenanigans."

"But..." Maddie protests.

"It's not made up!" I cut in.

"We didn't invent this!" Maddie adds.

"It's completely real! It actually happened!" I cry.

"Right, right..." the policeman said, rolling his eyes. "Would you, now, please leave this building? I would rather not have to escort you out. "

"Please, sir, this isn't a story! We're telling the truth!"

"Leave it to the trained professionals, young ladies."

"All right! When you find out we were right all along..." I threaten.

"And I can assure you that we won't. This is the third time I'm telling you to leave, and if I have to make it four, there will be consequences. You are forbidden to enter this institution to tell us about this story again until you have the jewels with you."

"ALL RIGHT!" Maddie shouts, raising her voice considerably. "WE'LL LEAVE, THEN!" And she takes me by the hand, dragging me out of the police department.

"That was completely pointless," I say to Maddie, as we stand outside the cinema once more, waiting for Uncle to come get us. "If only we'd actually had the jewels, then he would definitely have believed us."

"He might not have," Maddie contradicts. "He might have just come up with another way for it to not be real."

"S'pose that's true," I agree, sighing. What were we to do now?

At five thirty, Uncle drives up in his car. "Get in, girls!" He calls out the window. We walk to the car and get in, in silence.

"So, how was it?" Uncle inquires.

It takes me a moment to comprehend that he was referring to the cinema.

"It was good," I say. "The picture was amazing."

Maddie nods. "Yes, I enjoyed it too." And we left it at that.

"Wonderful. I can take you again if you would like. Maybe this weekend? That is, if you want to."

I agree, not really paying attention. The policeman had not believed our story. What would happen to the jewels now?

Maddie and I go to bed that evening very discouraged.

:876A#��

An Unexpected Visitor

T he following Tuesday morning, I wake up at 6:45, grinning. For a millisecond, I don't know why I'm so excited. Then it comes back to me.

It's my thirteenth birthday.

"Happy birthday, Elizabeth!!!"

Maddie (who has clearly been awake for quite a while, waiting for me to wake up) hurries over to my bed and tugs on my arm.

"Get up, get up, get up! Uncle's making you a special breakfast!" She squeals.

I almost spring out of bed. "A special breakfast?"

"Yes!" Maddie tells me excitedly. "He says that you get to choose what we have!"

"Really?" I hastily pull on my slippers and catapult downstairs, Maddie following.

Uncle emerges from the kitchen. "Happy birthday, Elizabeth! You're a teenager now!"

I hadn't yet thought of that. Yes, I was now a teenager. Thirteen. My grin widens.

"Thank you, Uncle."

"I assume Maddie has told you that you get to select our breakfast menu for today?" He smiles.

"Yes, she has," I tell him excitedly.

Uncle chuckles. "It'll have to be something I can whip up in twenty minutes. Middle school doesn't just stop happening on birthdays, you know." Maddie rolls her eyes, grinning.

"Er – can we just have bacon and eggs? I simply adore bacon."

"Absolutely. One large platter of bacon and eggs for the birthday girl, coming right up!" He grins once more and hurries back into the kitchen. He pauses on the threshold and turns back around.

"While I'm cooking, you two should get dressed."

"All right," I call after him. He goes back into the kitchen. Maddie and I dash back upstairs and get dressed. As soon as I've put on my favorite purple dress and combed my hair to celebrate what is to me the best day of the year, I race back downstairs and sit down at the table.

"Tuck your napkin into your front," Uncle reminds me. "I don't want you to get egg yolk on that nice dress. But you do look beautiful." I grudgingly tuck in my napkin like I am told, even though I look like I'm about four.

Maddie joins us, wearing a nice red dress to celebrate with me, just before Uncle serves the bacon and eggs. I listen to the inviting sound of the sizzling bacon in the pan as Uncle prods it occasionally, waiting for it to cook all the way. I notice that he doesn't tell Maddie to tuck her napkin into her front, and she doesn't do it herself. She simply puts it on her lap. I sigh. He clearly trusts Maddie to not spill more than he trusts me.

"Breakfast is served!" Uncle calls, brandishing a large plate covered in the aforesaid. He lays it down on the table. Maddie goes and collects forks and knives for everyone.

I begin by plunging my fork into the egg yolk, watching it seep into the bacon and egg white, which Uncle says is called the "albumen". I cut a small portion of the albumen, now covered in the yolk, and eat it. Then I pick up the bacon with my fingers. Uncle usually tells me to use a knife and fork to eat bacon, which is more difficult because bacon is hard to cut, but he doesn't. I suppose it's because today is my birthday. I try to conceal a small smile and crunch into the bacon, savoring that delightful, salty taste that I love so much.

"Have a wonderful day, girls," Uncle tells us later as he ushers us out the door. "And do try to keep those dresses clean," he adds. I pull on my favorite black coat that Uncle got me last year, swing my backpack strap over my shoulder, fix the laces on my shoes (I may be wearing a dress, but I'm still going to wear trainers, and that's that), and march out to the car.

"I can't believe you're actually thirteen," Maddie tells me as we buckle our seatbelts. "I'm going to be seventeen next month, though, which is amazing." She grins at me. "But, just for a month, we're technically only three years apart." Maddie's seventeenth birthday is on July seventh.

"That's funny, Maddie, you're going to be seventeen on the seventh of the seventh month."

"Oh, why yes, I hadn't thought of it like that." She smiles

We ride the rest of the way to school in thoughtful silence.

When we arrive, I am met with a pleasant surprise. Someone (i.e. Josie MacMillan) has stuck a piece of paper with the words "Happy birthday, Elizabeth!" on it, above a picture of balloons. I look over at locker 62. Josie is there, blushing furiously.

"Josie! There you are! Thanks so much for the note."

She turns around and pulls me into a hug. "Happy birthday!" She says. I smile.

"Thank you, Josie! Now let's go to History. Did you do the homework? I didn't understand question four..."

And we launch into normal conversation.

At the end of the day, Uncle pulls up in his car.

"How was school?" He inquires.

"Enjoyable. I wrote some more of the story I was doing in English class. And many people wished me a happy birthday."

We drive by Maddie's school. She has made a considerable amount of friends since September. Her best friend is called Elisa. Maddie strolls up, arm in arm with her, and gets in the car.

"Uncle, can we do presents when we get home?" Maddie asks. "I want to give Elizabeth mine."

Presents? I was surprised to get presents on Christmas, but on my birthday? The Earl never acknowledged our birthdays. In fact, when it was our birthday, he made us clean twice as much and he didn't let us have supper. He was, after all, a spiteful old git who turned out to be a criminal.

"Why, of course, Maddie. In fact, I have something to give your sister as well." He turns around, his eyes twinkling. Suddenly, he looks surprised.

"Oh, it's Queen Elizabeth's coronation today, isn't it? It's going to be on American television at seven o'clock. We can eat supper in front of the telly."

It is! I had forgotten. This made me sad. Queen Elizabeth was supposed to have a present from her sister Margaret Rose, but in fact, this present was in our attic. Not in England. I look at Maddie. We appear to both thinking the same thing.

When we arrive home, I immediately lead Maddie upstairs into our shared bedroom.

"Maddie, since the police won't believe us, we need to take matters into our own hands."

Maddie looks surprised at this.

"Meaning?"

"Meaning we need to write to the palace, tell them we have the jewels and also tell them exactly what happened, with Richard and Marissa and everything like that."

"Elizabeth..."

I know Maddie is angling for a counterargument, but nothing comes. She shakes her head slightly and sighs.

"I suppose we should, really. How else are they going to get back to England?"

I do not need to answer this; it is a rhetorical question. I fold my hands in my lap. We sit there for another few minutes before traipsing solemnly downstairs. Clearly Maddie doesn't want to write to the palace either. What if they didn't believe us? What if the jewels were lost on the way there, or were intercepted and stolen?

When we get downstairs, Uncle is sitting on the sofa with a huge grin on his face.

"Why are you so happy, Uncle?" I ask rather bluntly, without any preamble whatsoever. This results in a rather painful nudge in the ribs from Maddie. But Uncle doesn't seem to notice the impoliteness.

"Oh..." His grin widens. "I'm just pleased that my niece is thirteen."

I don't quite believe him. "Are you sure that's all?"

"I just feel rather in a good mood today. Or is that a crime now?" He laughs.

I frown. That surely can't be the only reason he is so jolly.

Maddie breaks the awkward moment by once again demanding that I open my presents.

"After supper, I should think," Uncle says, still grinning.

Maddie looks horrified. "So, after we watch the coronation, and every-thing?"

I shrug. "I really don't mind," I tell Uncle. "I never used to even get presents anyway. Maddie and I stopped receiving them in 1949."

Maddie continues to look horrified. "But, Uncle Henry..."

He cuts her off. "I'm sure it can wait until after supper," he repeats.

"I really don't mind at all," I say again.

Maddie looks grumpy but says nothing. We sit down on the sofa, but Uncle remains standing.

"Now," Uncle claps his hands together. "What for supper? How about... pork sandwiches, with loads of ketchup?"

Suddenly my sister looks rather surprised. I glance at her, curious.

"Yes, that would be wonderful," I tell Uncle, and he strolls gaily into the kitchen.

"What was that all about?" I ask Maddie.

Maddie looks misty-eyed. "Oh, nothing. It's just... pork sandwiches with ketchup was always... was always Dad's favorite."

I put on a pensive face. "I wonder why Uncle's making that."

"Maybe he likes it too. It probably doesn't matter, anyways."

We sit there, again in thoughtful silence.

"Dinner is served!" Uncle calls later, at 6:15. He brings out a tray of delicious-looking sandwiches. I grin. They really look delicious. He places them down on the coffee table, joining us on the sofa. "We'll put the television on at 6:50, all right?" He hands us all plates. "Serve yourselves. Three sandwiches maximum. And after the coronation, we can do cake and presents. Is that all right, Elizabeth?"

"Cake? You made me a cake?"

He laughs his rumbling laugh. "Of course I made you a cake! A birthday without cake? Preposterous! Let's have our sandwiches." He sits down, but he doesn't look very laid-back. He's sitting on the edge of the sofa, leaning forward.

"Uncle, is everything okay?"

"Okay? I'm not okay. I'm wonderful! I'm feeling really happy!" He rubs his hands together, still leaning forward. I frown. Something was up.

Suddenly, there's a knock on the door.

Uncle practically jumps out of his seat. He dashes over to the door. The blinds are drawn, so I can't see who it is.

"Who is it?" Uncle asks, even though it's perfectly clear that he already knows.

"It's me," says the door in a very slightly familiar voice.

Uncle opens the door. I am confused – "it's me" isn't any clarification as to who the person was. Clearly he had been expecting someone.

There's a middle-aged man standing on the threshold. His hair is a sandy brown, and it's in a shaggy state. He has a scraggly beard of the same color as well. His eyes are a brilliant shade of blue, and they have a slightly familiar twinkle in them that I can't quite lay a finger on. He looks rather windswept, as though he had just been on a long trip.

Maddie freezes, her sandwich halfway to her mouth. Her eyes widen, and she drops the sandwich. It clatters onto the plate. Her hands are still in their previous position. Then she almost falls off of the sofa, her arms whirling through space, her legs wriggling all around, as if she was being electrocuted. She ricochets over to the man standing grinning in the doorway. Then, to my absolute, utter surprise, she hugs him. I stare at her, also dropping my sandwich.

"Maddie! What are you doing?"

Maddie looks at me, still hugging the strange man. He's hugging her back, equally as tearful and happy.

She speaks in a very soft voice, her speech cracked. I can see a tear leaking out of her eye. Her cheeks are red.

"Elizabeth, don't you understand?"

"No, I don't. Who is this man?"

She speaks again, her voice still soft and cracked. Several tears of happiness are trickling down her face now.

"It's... oh, Elizabeth, it's Dad!"

I feel like a current of electricity is surging through my body. But I ignore it. I shake my head vigorously, staring at them.

"N-no. No. It isn't Dad. It can't be. It isn't Dad. It isn't. Dad went missing in action. He died. It isn't Dad, Maddie, it isn't! It isn't!" I have to convince myself that it isn't Dad, because if I let myself be lured into that trap of believing it's him, and then later find out that it isn't really him, my world would shatter.

Uncle gazes at me. I had forgotten that he was there.

"Elizabeth, it is your father. It's really, truly David Edward Murgatroyd, your father."

I don't know what to think. It couldn't be Dad. After eight whole years of the war being over? He would have come back before then. It was impossible.

I stare into the man's eyes. That twinkle...

Suddenly, I remember. Dad's eyes did twinkle like that.

"Dad," I whisper.

"Lizzy-B," he says back.

I laugh. "It's Elizabeth now, really."

And soon, I'm hugging Dad alongside Maddie, and he squeezes us back.

"Ten years," Dad whispers. "Ten whole years, and you were alive the whole time. And oh, how you've grown. Elizabeth, are you really thirteen today?

And Maddie, oh, Maddie, you're almost seventeen. You're both so grown up. I'm so sorry. I gave up too soon. Ever since I saw that that orphanage had been bombed..."

I wriggle out of Dad's strong arms, still holding his hand, and stare up at him.

"How? How did you find us? Where were you for eight years, after the war?"

Maddie looks up at Dad too.

"Yes, Dad, tell us what happened. We need to know."

Dad takes us by the hands and leads us back onto the sofa. Uncle sits next to us, but on the other side of Dad, so that we could be next to him.

"Ooh, you're having pork sandwiches with ketchup? My favorite!"

Maddie and I exchange glances. So Uncle had known. For how long had he known?

"It's rather a long story," Dad says. "Do you mind?"

"Not at all, David," Uncle says.

Dad takes a deep breath, and begins his story.

"Hitherto, I truly thought you both were dead. And I know you did too, after your reaction just now." We nod.

"Before I left for the war, I had an argument with Henry. I don't remember what it was about, but I know that it made us both very cross at each other." Dad and Uncle share a somber look.

"In 1944, I was taken into a prisoner-of-war camp in Germany, called Biebelsheim. I stayed there for a year and half. You probably got a telegram saying I was missing in action, did you not?" Maddie and I nod again, highly interested in what Dad had to say.

"Then the war was over, and we were released. I returned to England in 1946, only to find that our house had been destructed. Bomb, it looked like."

I have to blink back tears. "It was bombed?" I say softly.

"By the looks of it," Dad repeats. "I'm sorry, Elizabeth."

I look at Maddie again. She also looks sad.

"I knew that Mum and Granny were dead. I had a brief conversation with someone who lived nearby. He told me that you two had gone to an orphanage in Notting Hill. But when I showed up – it wasn't there. There was only a pit. It had also been bombed. I thought you were dead as well."

I watch Dad as he tells his tale. I feel sorry for him. He was finally released, only to discover that his entire family was supposedly dead?

Maddie opens her mouth to speak.

"But we evaded the catastrophe, Dad. Brilliant Elizabeth here" (at this, I blush) "saved both of our lives. She wanted to go outside. We were just down the street, and then there was a huge noise. We turned around, and the orphanage and everyone in it were reduced to rubble because of a huge explosive dropped by a fighter plane."

Dad raises his eyebrows. "So, if it weren't for clever Elizabeth, my girls wouldn't be here today?" He smiles.

"No," Maddie affirms.

I cut in. "Well, I wouldn't say that... really, it was just a bit of luck... I was only five at the time..."

"No, Elizabeth, you saved our lives."

I blush again, but don't argue. I suppose I did, in a way.

"All right, where was I? Ah, yes. Right after I found out that the orphanage was bombed, I tried to correspond with my apparent only remaining family member – Henry. So I wrote him a letter, to say sorry again for our argument. But I never got a reply, so I thought you were still cross."

At this, Uncle looks taken aback. "You sent me a letter?" He exclaims. "But I never received any letter!"

Dad seems surprised too. "You didn't? It must have gone missing, then! So you weren't angry anymore?"

"Of course I wasn't cross anymore. In fact, I was wondering myself if you were dead. But I didn't think of it much, because I was busy raising Charlie." Uncle looks at me sadly. "He would have been almost exactly your age, Elizabeth, if he was alive today. He was born in 1940 too." He sighs, clearly remembering his little son.

"I lived in a flat in London alone for years after that. But one day, very recently, only about two months ago, I met with a man in a coffee shop in Reading. I told him my name was David Murgatroyd, and he said he used to know a man named Murgatroyd – Henry Murgatroyd. So I told him that he was my brother, and he told me that your wife and son had perished." He looks at Uncle again. "So I wrote to you again, to share my condolences..."

"...and this time it got through. I was amazed. I thought for sure you were dead by then. It had been so long. So I wrote back, but all there was on the letter was a phone number so you could phone me up and have a proper conversation." The brothers smiled. Uncle kept on, this time addressing Maddie and I. "I told him I had his daughters, and, of course, your father was extraordinarily surprised."

I stare at Maddie. She stares back. So that was the truth about the mysterious phone call I had overheard Uncle having one night. When he said he had something, he was talking about Maddie and I. Not the jewels. And he was talking about coming to see us. That, at least, was cleared up. But Uncle had kept it a surprise for two weeks? The sly man! I grin.

Dad talks again. "So, naturally, I spent about a week packing up all my things and selling the flat, and then it took another week for me to take the boat here. I arrived two hours ago. I've brought this red suitcase" – Dad gestured to a suitcase next to the door that I had not noticed upon his arrival – "which contains a few things, and I shipped the rest of it out separately. It should arrive in two or three days."

Uncle nods. "You can have the spare room," he says. "It's right across the hall from the girls' room."

I gape at Dad. "You're... you're going to live with us, Dad?"

He laughs. "Of course I'm going to live with you! Did you think I was just visiting, or something? What a ridiculous idea! Yes, I'm going to live here with my daughters and my brother. Is that all right?" He adds, grinning boyishly.

I don't say anything but jump back into his arms, holding him tight.

"Don't ever leave me again, Dad," I whisper into his ear.

"I promise, I won't, for as long as I live."

The Coronation

- -

"These are really good sandwiches, Henry. Just how I like them; loads and loads and loads of ketchup." He chuckles. "A lovely welcome-back gift." He licks the stray ketchup off his mouth.

"The coronation'll be playing now," Uncle says suddenly. "We should put it on."

"Oh, yes," Maddie cried.

Uncle pulled back the black tarp covering the television, snatched up something called a remote control, which controlled the television, and pressed a button. The screen fuzzed for a few minutes, and then the picture became clear. Queen Elizabeth was sitting on a throne in Westminster Abbey, wearing her glorious, huge crown and her jewel-bedecked robes. She had clearly just been crowned. The choir was singing. She looked rather somber. I suppose the crown must be very heavy.

We watched the procession, enraptured. Then, at the end, came Elizabeth's coronation speech.

"Throughout this memorable day," said the television Queen Elizabeth, "I have been uplifted and sustained by the knowledge that your thoughts and prayers were with me. I have been aware all the time that my peoples, spread far and wide throughout every continent and ocean in the world, were united to support me in the task to which I have now been dedicated with such solemnity."

Queen Elizabeth's speech was very true. Even though we were not in England, watching the coronation there, we were still supporting her, supporting her reign over the United Kingdom, whilst being far away in America.

"Many thousands of you came to London from all parts of the Commonwealth and Empire to join in the ceremony, but I have been conscious too of the millions of others who have shared in it by means of wireless or television in their homes. All of you, near or far, have been united in one purpose. It is hard for me to find words in which to tell you of the strength of which this knowledge has given me."

"That's us," Maddie says. "We are among the 'millions of others who have shared in it by means of wireless or television in their homes'."

I nod in agreement.

Queen Elizabeth's speech was quite long, but very uplifting.

"As this day draws to its close, I know that my abiding memory of it will be, not only the solemnity and beauty of the ceremony, but the inspiration of your loyalty and affection. I thank you all from a full heart. God bless you all."

And it was ended at that.

"That was incredible," Dad said. "So inspiring. I really can't believe that she's queen. She's an amazing woman."

Uncle suddenly looks sober. "Did you hear that one of the presents that Princess Margaret was going to give the queen for her coronation day has gone missing?" He tells Dad.

"No, I hadn't!" Dad exclaims. "What was the present?"

"A ruddy chest full of jewels, I think. Necklaces, things like that."

Maddie's cheeks are glowing red, and I can tell that mine are too.

"Erm... about that..." Maddie begins.

Dad looks puzzled. "Yes, Maddie?"

"Weknowexactlywherethejewelsareandwhostolethem," I rattle off at top speed, as if saying it fast would make it easier to say.

Uncle jumps up. "WHAT? You girls know where stolen jewels are?"

I sigh. "It's a really, really long story."

Dad's eyebrows are creased. "You were never the type to lie. Why did you come up with this story?"

Maddie and I are both infuriated. Was Dad going to be just like the idiot police officer? I suppose he really doesn't know us very well...

"We're not lying, Dad. Really. We wouldn't lie about this! That would be ridiculous!"

Uncle looks cross. "All right then. If you really know where they are, then show us," he exclaims in an unusually harsh voice that I haven't really heard before. His tone also drips with sarcasm.

I look at him matter-of-factly. "Okay, we will. Just first listen to our story."

Dad and Uncle share a glance. I can tell they're both thinking the same thing – all right... let's humor them. See if they do have these jewels.

Maddie begins. "Well, it all started on the very night we arrived, just after Marissa left..."

And we begin telling Uncle and Dad the whole story of the mystery.

"– I went into the attic, even though I wasn't supposed to – yes, sorry, Uncle – and I found that very ruddy chest of jewels. I couldn't believe it. I told Maddie. We thought they had been stolen..."

"– That very night, Elizabeth and I went back into the attic – all right, yes, it was extremely late, we know – and while we were up there, I found a note from Prince Phillip. Prince Phillip! It was addressed to Margaret Rose, saying that they were to be presents to her sister. And, we regret it now, yes, but we both thought it was you, Uncle Henry, who had stolen them. Why else would they be in your house?"

Uncle cuts in, sighing. "Yes, well, I suppose you had the right to think that."

We carried on.

"– I showed them to my friend Molly, and one of the necklaces was missing. Also, the chest of jewels had been moved to your cabinet, Dad" – I point to the cabinet that Dad had made – "and were put in a secret compartment..."

"– when you, Uncle, were out, and there were footsteps leading away from the attic window..."

The story goes on and on, Uncle and Dad looking more and more surprised and awed – and cross – with every word.

When we start talking about me being kidnapped, Uncle and Dad are outraged.

"YOU WERE SICK, AND GOT KIDNAPPED? BY MARISSA?"

I look down at my hands, my face heating up. "Erm... yes. That's pretty... pretty much it."

The two of them look highly indignant, but say nothing. We continue with the story.

We finally get to the bit about last Monday.

"– So... we... sort of... snuck in last Monday when we were off school..."

Uncle seems quite cross, but also mildly impressed.

"You broke into Marissa's house? So by then, you had established that it had to be either Oscar or Marissa?"

I sighed. Why didn't they understand? "We knew it was Marissa, Uncle. She had the same eyes as the thief, her shoes were the same as the prints we saw leading away from the attic, and it was the same house I had been taken to when I was kidnapped."

"All right, so you broke into Marissa's house, knowing it was Marissa, and then what happened?"

"We were... erm... looking for the jewels, and then I saw Marissa driving up in her car. We hid in the closet. She came into her room, started listening to music..."

"So, hang on – Marissa is secretly a notorious villain? I'm not buying it."

"Oh, for goodness' sake, Uncle, just hear us out!" I cry.

"All right, all right, go on, then."

"We ran out of the room in the nick of time, but Marissa saw Maddie, and I think me as well, but she had a plan, I guess, so Maddie had to pretend she was here to retrieve a coat she had left there on Saturday. Then we looked for ages, and found the jewels cleverly disguised in a bowl of

sweets. Except the sapphire necklace wasn't among them, so we had to look further. Maddie made a noise downstairs to distract her, while I rifled through her things."

"You looked through her things?"

Maddie rolls her eyes. "Yes, of course, we had to find the necklace! I thought she had decided to keep it for herself. But then Marissa realized that I was the source of the noise and told me to get out, so I left, but later climbed back up the big tree we had used to get in. Elizabeth was still there."

Uncle and Dad are frowning. I start talking again.

"Marissa came back upstairs, so I hid in the cupboard in her bedroom once again, but then I had to sneeze, and that revealed me. She found me, took a firm grip on my arm so I couldn't go, and said she was very cross, and she was going to... to tie me up again, like she had before, and then she told me the craziest thing." I didn't want to tell Uncle and Dad that she had threatened to chain me up, so I didn't specify whether she wanted to tie me with chains or ropes. But I thought "tie" generally implied that it was ropes, and I dearly hoped that that's what they would think.

"What? What did she tell you?" Dad asks, indignant.

"She revealed that... it wasn't all her. That... that she was only an accomplice. She..."

Maddie comes to my rescue. She knows I don't want to say it in front of Uncle.

"She told Elizabeth that Richard Grayson was actually behind it, and he had used us to smuggle the jewels to America. She said that she wasn't there that first night to make new friends in the neighborhood, she was there to retrieve the jewels from our bags. Richard Grayson works at Buckingham Palace, and he took the jewels right before he left one night."

Uncle jumps up from the sofa, staring at Maddie with a look on his face of shock and disgrace.

"WHAT? That awful man who was your guardian in England? He is the reason for this?"

Dad, however, looks puzzled.

"Who's Richard Grayson?"

I groan. "He was our guardian in England when we thought you were dead, Dad. After the bomb hit the orphanage, we were on the streets, and then a woman called Charlotte Grayson came to adopt us. She was very nice, but married to Richard Grayson. After four years, she died, and Richard started being wicked to us, making us do all the housework, not sending us to school, and being downright cruel all the time – not celebrating our birthdays, occasionally shutting us in our rooms for several days as a punishment, taping our mouths shut at night... and then we realized that he was a horrid miscreant."

Dad's arms are folded tight across his chest, and he is rocking back and forth on the rocking armchair.

"You were in England the whole time... and this terrible villain was your guardian... whereabouts did you live?"

"Kew Gardens," Maddie says softly. "You know, it's on the district line of the tube, near Earl's Court."

Our father's lips are pursed. "So close... and I never knew..."

Uncle intervenes loudly, trying to break the awkward moment.

"What happened after Marissa told you that?"

Maddie begins again. "I gestured to Elizabeth from outside, pointing to Marissa's neck, because I had seen the sapphire necklace we were looking for hanging there. Elizabeth unlatched the window that the tree branch I was sitting on led towards, and I jumped in... um... and I..."

"Maddie's feet flew into Marissa, and it broke her hip. It was fabulous. It bled loads, so we had a great advantage and ran all the way home. I was so glad; Marissa had said she was going to kill me. She said she only told me all those things about the mystery because she planned to dispose of me later. We ran home with the jewels."

Uncle's expression is practically unreadable. I determine that it is one of mingled fury, surprise, relief, sadness, and praise. Dad just looks overwhelmingly proud.

"You broke her hip?" Dad asks. "That's amazing. I know, I know, it must have been awful for her, but she was threatening to kill you, so I suppose you're eligible for injuring." He grins. Uncle looks a bit put off at Dad's simple dismissal of Maddie's mishap, and learning that his daughter was threatened with death, but doesn't say anything.

"And that's it," Maddie says, her confidence returning.

"So you kept this a secret from any adults this whole time."

"Oh, actually, no, we forgot to tell you – we went to the police after we saw the cinema Tuesday afternoon. They didn't believe us. We were going to write to the palace about it."

Uncle is frowning again.

"Hang on – you said you knew exactly where the jewels were. Where are they, then?"

I exhale. After the story, something nobody would make up to their own parents, they finally believed us. "They're... they're in the attic. Our attic."

Dad stands up quickly. "Well, what are you waiting for? Go get them!"

Maddie and I dash upstairs. I snatch up the ladder, propping it against the trapdoor. Maddie clambers up first, and I follow close behind. She dashes over to the chest, which we had hidden behind a cardboard box full of old cushions. I run over to her and grab the rusty-red chest, feeling the smooth wood and breathing in the smell it emitted. We seal the trapdoor behind us as we race back downstairs to join Uncle and Dad once again.

"Here it is," says Maddie, and I hand them the chest. We had left it un-locked.

Dad takes it, gently clicking open the latch. The jewels are there, as shiny as ever. Dad runs his hands over them, mesmerized as I was when I first found them.

"They're... beautiful," he whispers.

I carefully prize the chest from Dad's hands, rummaging through the jewels. I finally find the torn note from Phillip to Margaret.

"Here's the note," I say, tossing it to Uncle. "See? It's signed by Prince Phillip. It was torn by Marissa, but she didn't throw it away, which is good."

Uncle looks amazed.

"I didn't fully believe you up until now," he says. "But you've proven you did all of that with this chest – how long did it take for you to solve all of this?"

I am irritated. Uncle didn't believe us until we showed him proof. But, nonetheless, I try to stay nonchalant. Maddie answers his question for me.

"Erm... we started the day we arrived, and we've been working on it rather solidly up until we solved it last Monday."

I raise my eyebrows. "Solidly? You were the one who was saying we should call it off."

She looks at me. "Well, yes, all right... we solved a lot in August and September, and then we came to a dead end... so we didn't really do it up until Elizabeth was kidnapped in May. That was about nine months of not working on it. We had no leads. But then Elizabeth was taken, and got away, so she knew where the thief's house was, and then we figured out that it was Marissa's house."

"She was going to murder me, Maddie. Marissa should keep a better eye on her prisoners. She had her back to me, and was blasting loud music, so I was able to slip out. She's also not very good at running, I was outrunning her already before I locked her in."

"Girls, I'm really, really, really proud of you," Uncle says. I smile. "This sounds terribly difficult, and you both narrowly escaped death." Yup, I think. Especially me. "But really, next time, leave it to the adults. Twelve- and sixteen-year-olds shouldn't be involved in this sort of thing."

I stop smiling and roll my eyes. I knew this was what he was going to say. "First of all, Uncle, I'm thirteen now. And second of all, the perfect, amazing adults had no idea whatsoever where to start with this mystery! We were the ones who were right in the middle of all the action."

Uncle looks rather unprepared for this outburst. But I was quite cross. Why does nobody trust young people to do these sorts of things? Leave it to the adults... let a grown-up do it... we can handle it better... et cetera...

"You could have at least mentioned that priceless jewels were in our attic, couldn't you?"

Dad steps in. "Henry! Elizabeth! Stop arguing." He suddenly sniffs the air eagerly. "Is that birthday cake I smell?"

Maddie jumps up. "Ooh, yes, let's have the cake! And then I can give Elizabeth my present!"

Uncle smiles. "That sounds like a good idea." He seems glad that the short disagreement is over.

"What kind of cake is it, Uncle?" Maddie asks.

"Chocolate cake," he says. "With a ton of icing. I seem to remember David loving icing..."

"Fabulous, I love chocolate!" Dad exclaims. "Especially chocolate icing. A wonderful combination of deliciousness."

"I don't remember the last time we had chocolate. Do you, Maddie?"

She shakes her head. "Although I'm certain we've had it before."

Dad looks outraged. "You don't remember when you last had chocolate? You must have had some chocolate after I left."

"Well... I think it was an occasional special treat at the orphanage... and Charlotte would give us some for the holidays sometimes... but Richard..." My voice fades away. I don't need to go on, anyways – it's obvious to everyone present that Richard Grayson would never be so kind as to even think of giving us something sweet, let alone a delicacy like chocolate.

Dad shook his head. "I can't believe this. You've been awfully mistreated. I mean, annoying chores and things, yes, but no chocolate?"

"None whatsoever. As a result, neither of us really have a very sweet tooth anymore," Maddie says.

"Isn't it unbelievable, Henry? The girls don't remember the last time they had chocolate."

But Uncle Henry isn't in the room anymore. He's gone into the kitchen to fetch the cake.

Suddenly, the lights are off.

"Uncle! Why did you turn the lights off?" I ask.

In response to my question, Uncle walks carefully into the room, carrying a decadent, three-tiered chocolate cake lathered in chocolate icing. Thirteen glowing candles have been placed in a circle on the top tier.

Uncle, Dad, and Maddie begin singing a birthday song that I've never heard before. Presumably, Maddie remembers it from when Mum and Dad lived with us.

I suddenly find that I'm grinning so wide my mouth is beginning to hurt.

"Happy birthday to you..."

I put my arm around Maddie.

"Happy birthday to you..."

Maddie puts her arm around me.

"Happy birthday, dear Elizabeth..."

We grin at each other.

"Happy birthday to... youuuuuuuuuuuu!!!!"

Uncle places the cake on the coffee table in front of me.

"Blow out the candles and make a wish," he whispers into my ear.

I puff as hard as I can onto the candles on top. Twelve of them extinguish in one blow. The last one shudders a bit, but stays aflame.

I blow on the last candle. It goes out.

I make a wish.

My family erupt into applause and cheers. Dad claps me on the back. Maddie hugs me.

"Did you make a wish?" She asks me eagerly. I nod.

"Ooh, what did you wish for?"

I am about to tell her, but Dad puts his hand on my shoulder.

"Never give away what you wished for, Elizabeth, or it won't come true."

"Why not?" I ask.

"Because it's the rules," Dad says vaguely, shrugging.

"Sorry, Maddie."

"I'll go fetch a knife and some plates, shall I?" Uncle says. He bustles back into the kitchen, returning with a rather sharp kitchen knife and four paper plates that he appears to have pre-purchased for the occasion.

I stare eagerly at the cake as Dad slices through it, readying myself for the sweet taste I know is waiting for me. The lush, gooey chocolate looks outstanding.

Dad places a huge slice on one of the plates and hands it to me.

"You can eat it with your hands," he says to me. "But mind you wash them after. Oh, and here's a napkin." I begrudgingly put the napkin on the table. He's reminding me a bit of Uncle this morning.

My slice has a candle sticking out of the top. I recognize it to be the obstinate candle that refused to be blown out on the first go. It was pink. I smile and pull it out, licking the icing off the bottom.

It was the most amazing luxury I had experienced in a very, very long time. Better than root beer and ice cream, for those were too sweet.

I carefully pick up the cake, getting icing all over my fingers, and swallow the whole thing in what seems like two seconds.

Uncle looks over me, laughing. I notice he is only a couple bites into his cake. He's eating it with a fork.

"Gosh, Elizabeth, you practically inhaled that cake. Would you like some more?"

"Oh, go on then," I say casually, giggling, as if I wasn't already craving seconds. Uncle cuts me another slightly smaller piece, placing it on my plate.

I sink my teeth into the sticky dessert, sighing with pleasure as it gently slides down my throat.

Maddie has finished with her piece. For once, Maddie has embraced her inner child and eaten with her hands.

"Dad, can I go fetch my present for Elizabeth?"

"Ah, yes, this is the perfect time for presents. And Henry, you should probably go get yours too. Mine is outside."

Maddie dashes upstairs, returning with a quite small, rectangular box wrapped in blue paper. She seats herself back down on the sofa with the present on her lap, affectionately squeezing my arm.

Uncle slowly makes his way to his room upstairs as well, returning with a box only slightly larger than the one Maddie is holding. His is wrapped in red paper.

"Where's your present, Dad?" Maddie asks.

"Oh, I'll get it in a bit. I'm afraid if I bring it inside, it'll give away the contents before Elizabeth has even opened it."

Uncle looks a little bit confused.

"All right, then, let's start with me, then we can do Maddie, and then we can do your father."

Uncle hands me his gift. I excitedly tear the wrapping off. I am left with a little brown box, which I gently pull the lid off of.

Nestled in the box is a gleaming red wristwatch. The black little ticking hands are pointing to the numbers on the side. There is an intricate golden design around the edge of the watch face.

"Uncle, this is amazing. Thank you so, so, much." I examine the watch further. "Wait – it says the time is half past six. That can't be right."

"You're very welcome, Elizabeth. It isn't six thirty, you're right. It's about a quarter past eight. That watch shall need winding." He points to a little gold knob on the side. "I'll do it for you, hand it here." I pass the watch to Uncle. The grin on my face feels like it's stuck.

"Ooh, let me give Elizabeth my present now." Maddie says eagerly. She's practically bouncing up and down on the sofa.

"Of course, go ahead," Dad says, visibly amused.

Maddie hands me her box. I carefully remove the paper, taking care not to tear it. I do not consciously know why I am doing this.

Inside is a little woven bracelet almost identical to the one currently tied around Maddie's wrist, but much, much cleaner. The bracelet is blue with small threads of violet woven into it. I examine it, holding it delicately in my hands and beaming at Maddie.

"It's so we can match," Maddie says in a quiet voice.

By now, more tears are streaking down my face.

"Just – just like the one that M-Mum made f... for you," I splutter with difficulty. The tears are restricting my speech.

"Yes," Maddie says, still whispering. "I made it myself. I hope you like it."

"It's... it's perfect," I tell her. "Thank you, thank you so much."

"So people know we are sisters."

"Yes. Sisters we are. Forever."

After Maddie and I are finished with our sister moment, Dad cuts in once again.

"That is a truly wonderful gift, Maddie. Really, really thoughtful. It must have taken you ages to make that. And it really looks just like the one that Mum made for you."

Maddie smiles.

By this point, Uncle has finished adjusting the time on my new watch.

"Here you go, Elizabeth." He snaps it around my right wrist. I wave my hand through the air, examining it and getting used to having it on.

"It's smashing, Uncle. Fabulous. I really like it."

"I'm glad." He smiles.

I pick up the bracelet that Maddie has just given me and slip it on my left wrist. It looks pretty there. I touch it, twirling it around on my arm. Maddie watches me, smiling.

"Well, Elizabeth, I have a present for you now, and I think you're going to like it." Dad smiles mysteriously and heads outside.

He returns with a rather large cardboard box. The box isn't wrapped. Dad seems to stagger with the contents of the box, which seems bizarre. The box doesn't appear to be exceedingly heavy. I notice something different about the box. Something in the sides. Something that looks a little bit like... tiny holes?

Air holes.

The cogs in my brain begin turning again, but before all of the rust can be cleaned off of them, Dad has handed me the box and I open it with a small knife.

The contents of the box leap out onto my lap and smile at me.

It's a little gray kitten. A kitten with fur the color of moonshine, and eyes as green as fresh grass. The kitten licks her paw in a thoughtful way, and then takes off from my lap and bounds around the room, sniffing in every corner, prodding everything with her paw (even Uncle's prized golden statue, which he was visibly slightly irritated about) and investigating as much as she could.

"Dad, you got me a kitten?!"

"Yes, Elizabeth, I got you a kitten. Do you like her?"

"She's perfect! Absolutely perfect!" I cry.

Maddie is watching the kitten as she plays, giggling. "I love cats. She's adorable. Her fur seems so soft."

"Where did you get her?" I ask, still watching the kitten.

"Uncle gave me a heads-up about bringing a present," Dad says, "so I looked around the shops in Notting Hill for a bit, until I came to a boy about eighteen selling kittens. He had the mother on the table next to him. It appeared that his cat had given birth to a litter of kittens that he needed to sell. So I said I'd take the smallest one. She cost me less than a shilling. I took her on the boat with me. Oh, and there's something else in the box, too. Not very exciting."

I reach my hand into the box. Sitting in the back is a rather squashed lily flower. I take it out.

"Why the lily?" I ask.

"The boy was giving out free lilies for all the cat purchasers. So I took one. Sorry, I know it's a bit crumpled."

I finger the petals of the lily thoughtfully.

"I've got it," I suddenly say.

"What?" Maddie asks, confused.

"I know what I'm going to call her."

"What's that?" Dad asks, beaming at the kitten. He looked pleased with his ability to make me so happy while barely knowing me.

"Lily. I'll call her Lily, because of the lily flower."

"That's a lovely name," Uncle says. "She's a very sweet cat."

"Lily! Come here, Lily."

Lily stops sniffing and turns to look at me. Her expression seems pensive for a moment, and then she bounds over to where I am sitting, bumping her head against my front. I scratch her behind the ears, smiling.

"I think she already knows her name," I say, laughing. "Her fur is so soft."

"Hello, Lily. You are a beautiful little kitten," Maddie coos. Lily jumps over to Maddie, letting her pet her. "I was right. She really is soft." She hands her back to me, and I cradle the kitten in my arms, still smiling.

"Elizabeth? Maddie?"

"Yes?" I ask. We're sitting together, stroking and petting Lily.

"What exactly do you plan to do with these royal jewels?" Dad asks.

The jewels are still sitting on the coffee table, twinkling in the light from above.

"Er –" I begin, not really knowing how to continue.

"We, erm, were going to write to the palace about them," Maddie says.

"That doesn't sound like a great idea. The Queen gets so much mail – especially right around the coronation – and she has no time to read all of them. It's highly likely she'll never read yours."

"If we write 'URGENT' and 'PLEASE READ' on the front she might," I argue.

"I don't think so, Elizabeth. We should give the police department a call. I will. You know what, I'll do it right now."

I raise my eyebrows, intrigued. Uncle dashes upstairs to the telephone in the hall. I hear him dialing, and then I can hear what he's saying.

"Police department? Yes. My name is Henry Murgatroyd, and I have the stolen chest of jewels. No, oh my goodness, of course I didn't steal them, do you think I would be telling you my name if I was the thief? Let me tell you what happened. A man named Richard Grayson and his sister Marissa are responsible..."

I lean back in my seat, smiling to myself. I suppose after all of this, the police are only going to believe the adults. I think back to my twelfth birthday last year. I remember it vividly. The Earl woke me up at the crack of dawn, telling me he wanted me to clean the entire downstairs before midday. This was highly unfair, because I had cleaned the whole house the day before. But I grudgingly cleaned, and then when midday came, the Earl found a clump of dust lying in a corner and said that I had done a horrible job cleaning and that I wasn't going to get any lunch. So he made me watch as he and Maddie ate some baked beans (Maddie's portion was much, much smaller than the Earl's), and in the afternoon, I had to clean the whole living room again, because that's where he found the clump of dust (although I have a suspicion that he might have planted that there himself). And for supper, I had a bit of canned tuna that had expired. It made me vomit all over my carpet later, which I had to clean up all by myself, and the next day, I got in a load of trouble because of the stain that was left. I remember the night of my twelfth, thinking to myself Oh yeah. I'm twelve. Huh.

I never could have thought, on my twelfth birthday, that the next year, I would be in America, I would have just solved a mystery, I would be living with my Uncle (who really wasn't bad at all)...

I would have four new friends...

I would have a kitten...

Dad would have just come home...

I snap out of my reverie as Uncle raises his voice during the phone call.

"My niece was kidnapped, all right? Those villains need to be arrested!" Pause. "Two nieces. And, might I add, they solved the whole thing, being in the center of death threats, being tied up, blah, blah, blah... Anyway, the point is, you have to believe me." Pause. "Elizabeth and Madeleine. Elizabeth is the younger. They were the girls who came to your department last week. You should have believed them. I'll come down with the jewels tomorrow." Another pause. "Okay, I agree, but what's proof when my girls were in the center of everything? I can bring my girls down tomorrow if I have to, they have legitimate accounts of what happened. Three? That works? Okay. Thank you so much for believing my incredulous story." I hear the click of the phone and then footsteps on the stairs.

"Well, that's that. As I'm sure you all heard, I'm to meet them at three with the jewels and you, Elizabeth – sorry, Maddie, but Elizabeth was the one who saw Marissa and all that." I grin. "Shall I go fetch some champagne, David?" He adds to Dad.

"Go on, then," he replies, grinning.

Maddie suddenly stands up.

"I'll be right back," she says. "I have to go to the loo."

Only Dad, Lily and I remain. Dad pulls me closer.

"Do you remember, Elizabeth, when I left for the war, how I told you I was going to come back? How I told you to never give up hope? How – how I told you to wait for me?"

I do remember this. I remember this very well.

"Yes," I say softly.

"Did you? Did you believe I would return?"

"In the back of my mind, I still hoped. But I never really thought – after so long..."

"Well... I can't blame you for that. But I feel awful. I've missed out on ten years of your childhood. I've missed out on the majority of your growth. You're just going to get bigger now. You were just beginning to speak when I left, and now you're practically a grown-up. I missed out on having a sweet little girl running about. I barely know you, Elizabeth. We were just starting to figure out your personality. And now, it's as if you skipped ten years and became a teenager! You went from toddler to teenager. Never were you a child to me."

"I didn't know who I was myself up until recently. I was never allowed alone time after the age of five, when the orphanage was bombed. I was always with Richard and Maddie, and up until 1949, Charlotte. I barely ever got to read, because I love to read, and I barely ever got to draw, because I also love to draw. I had to clean all the time when Charlotte died. And when she was alive, we didn't have many more privileges but we were allowed books and didn't have to clean so much. All Charlotte did was homeschool us. I was so bored. I've done enough cleaning to last me a lifetime, and Maddie's done more."

"I'm so glad to have you back. You have no idea what I was like when I found out you girls were alive. I cried so much I thought I would shrivel up. I must have sounded so funny on the other end of the phone." He emits a rather odd laugh.

We hug for what seems like a million years. Uncle comes back with the champagne and places it on the coffee table. We break apart at his return, rather abruptly.

"Sorry to interrupt this father-daughter moment," he says, "but I know that you love this kind of champagne, David. And I think I have some sparkling apple juice for my grown-up nieces. It looks a bit like beer." He chuckles.

Maddie returns from the loo and sits by me. I am absent-mindedly patting Lily, deep in thought. Once Maddie begins speaking, though, I listen very hard. Maddie's looking ahead, as if the thing she has to say is easier to admit without making eye-contact with me.

"Do you know, Elizabeth, I'm really proud of you. If it weren't for you, the jewels would be at Marissa's house right now, and she would have won. You were excellent, really excellent."

"Thanks, Maddie. You were amazing too, you know. Saving my life and stuff."

"And stuff," Maddie repeats, laughing a bit. Now she looks at me. "I'm sorry I called you irresponsible after you were kidnapped. That must have been utterly traumatizing, and I bet you didn't need me shouting at you after."

"That's okay. I shouted at you too. And anyway, you noticed the sweet bowl in the first place. I hadn't seen it, I was looking for the jewels elsewhere. And you can't deny that you saved both of our lives by breaking Marissa's hip and getting us out of there with all the jewels."

She leans against me, and takes my hand. "I'm really lucky to have you as a sister, Elizabeth."

"And I you, Maddie."

"I never could have made it through those horrible years with the Earl if I hadn't had you with me."

"Neither could I," I agree. "You're the best friend anyone could ever have."

"I hope we stay with Uncle and Dad forever."

"We will. Don't worry about that."

"Do you girls want some sparkling juice, or not?"

"Of course we do, Uncle!"

He pours us two glasses and hands them to us.

"Thank you," Maddie says.

Dad is now having a third glass of champagne. His cheeks are red; not from blushing, not from anger, but from drinking. The brothers are chuckling and hiccupping and toasting over and over. I take a sip from my cup. The fizziness reminds me of the root beer, but otherwise it tastes just like apples. Sweetened apples.

"Shall we make a proper toast, now that we all have drinks?" Uncle calls across the coffee table.

"Yes, let's," Maddie agrees.

"To Elizabeth," Dad calls.

"To Elizabeth," everyone else repeats, and, blushing, I clink my glass with theirs. Then we sip.

"To Dad, for coming home!" Maddie shouts.

"To Dad," Maddie and I say, and Uncle says "To David." We all tap glasses again. Another sip.

"To the Murgatroyds," says Dad, and we all repeat, laughing and clinking and sipping and chuckling.

I finish the rest of my glass, pour myself more, and drink it again. I don't remember the last time I was so happy.

Do you want to know what I wished for when I blew out my candles?

I thought so.

I wished for many things.

I wished that Marissa and Richard would be apprehended and sentenced to a long time in prison.

I wished that Queen Elizabeth would eventually receive her present.

I wished that we would get some credit for solving all of it.

I wished that Dad would be with us forever.

I wished that my life would stay as good as it is right now.

I wished that I would always have my sister.

My sister nudges me.

"Happy birthday, Elizabeth." I look over at her and smile.

I look around at everyone. I look at Uncle Henry, who turned out to be the best uncle anyone could ever ask for. At Maddie, my partner in crime and the most amazing sister in the world. At Lily, who has now fallen asleep against my leg.

At Dad.

And as I look at all of these incredible people, I realize that it really is wonderful to be Elizabeth Murgatroyd.

Epilogue

TWO MONTHS LATER

"Elizabeth? Maddie? You might want to see this..."

The Murgatroyd sisters heard their father calling upstairs to them. They raced down to see him holding a newspaper in his hands, beaming at it. He noticed their arrival and laid it down on the coffee table.

"Read," he said.

The headline was, in big bold letters: TWO GIRLS PLAY DETECTIVE AND SOLVE THE MOST IMPORTANT CASE OF THE YEAR.

The sub-head read: Teen girls find missing English royal jewels before police department even knows which continent to look in.

Elizabeth and Maddie shared a glance.

"You got credit," called their uncle from the other side of the room. The girls hadn't noticed him there. "Like you wanted."

Maddie read the article first, then handed it to her sister to read. The highlights of the article were as follows:

Richard Grayson is currently in a high-security penitentiary awaiting trial (his sister Marissa, an accomplice, was found dead by her boyfriend Oscar Jones on her sofa with a severely fractured hip which caused her to die of blood loss. Madeleine Murgatroyd is said to have kicked her, which caused the hip fracture, but the death was caused by running four blocks with her injury).

Misses Madeleine and Elizabeth Murgatroyd shall be receiving medals of Honor in two days' time from the Long Island Police Department as a reward for all their trouble.

Queen Elizabeth received the full, undamaged chest of jewels from her sister after they were specially shipped to her from New York.

"Well, there you have it," said David. "Medals of Honor... oh, I'm so proud of my daughters." Henry nodded in agreement.

"What? Marissa died?" Elizabeth said, surprised. "You practically killed her, Maddie!"

Maddie's face went a deep shade of red. She said nothing.

David and Henry ignored this statement.

"Girls – school starts soon. Shall I take you shopping this weekend? For new clothes, things like that?" Henry added.

"Sure," Maddie said. "Sounds great." She turned to her sister. "You ready for eighth grade? Oldest one in middle school. You'll be in high school with me before you know it."

Elizabeth looked elated. "That's right! And eighth grade... I feel much less nervous this year, though, now that I have Josie and everyone else."

"Yeah, I have my friend Lindsey now. The only other nerd in the whole school."

"Wow."

"Come on, sis. Hey, you know those books Uncle got me, by the mystery writer Agatha Christie? They're really good, much better than the Famous Five. Much more mature. You should read them."

"Yeah, I will. And we should take the paper." Elizabeth picked it up.

The girls ran back upstairs. David looked after them, smiling and shaking his head.

"They're so grown up, I can't believe it. I'm still not used to it, even after being back for a while now."

"That's what happens to kids, Davy," sighed Henry, resorting back to his old nickname for his brother. "They grow up. They become independent. Every day their independence grows. They're growing into beautiful young women."

"I know. And I don't like it."

"That's life, little bro."

David laughed.

"Yeah. I suppose it is. My girls..."

He sighed happily.

"My girls."